ONE-PUNCH FARGO

Slade kept the scattergun lowered at the piano as the entire saloon froze.

"You might want to get out of the way," he said. "That thing's likely to come apart like a one-hoss shay."

"I don't think so," Fargo said, being close enough to Slade to do something about him.

Slade started to turn to see who was talking to him, and Fargo helped him out. He grabbed Slade's shoulder and spun him, knocking the shotgun barrel up with his left arm and slamming his right fist into the man's solar plexus, striking like an iron mallet. Slade's eyes widened in pain as his breath left him. He dropped the shotgun, and the Trailsman caught it before it hit the floor, clicked back both hammers, and pressed it against Slade's thick skull. . . .

THE TRAILSMAN #249

SILVER CITY SLAYER

by

Jon Sharpe

A SIGNET BOOK

SIGNET
Published by New American Library, a division of
Penguin Putnam Inc., 375 Hudson Street,
New York, New York 10014, U.S.A.
Penguin Books Ltd, 80 Strand,
London WC2R 0RL, England
Penguin Books Australia Ltd, Ringwood,
Victoria, Australia
Penguin Books Canada Ltd, 10 Alcorn Avenue,
Toronto, Ontario, Canada M4V 3B2
Penguin Books (N.Z.) Ltd, 182–190 Wairau Road,
Auckland 10, New Zealand

Penguin Books Ltd, Registered Offices:
Harmondsworth, Middlesex, England

First published by Signet, an imprint of New American Library,
a division of Penguin Putnam Inc.

First Printing, July 2002
10 9 8 7 6 5 4 3 2 1

The first chapter of this title originally appeared in *Arizona Ambush*,
the two hundred forty-eighth volume in this series.

Ⓤ REGISTERED TRADEMARK—MARCA REGISTRADA

Printed in the United States of America

PUBLISHER'S NOTE
This is a work of fiction. Names, characters, places, and incidents either are
the product of the author's imagination or are used fictitiously, and any
resemblance to actual persons, living or dead, events, or locales is entirely
coincidental.

The Trailsman

Beginnings . . . they bend the tree and they mark the man. Skye Fargo was born when he was eighteen. Terror was his midwife, vengeance his first cry. Killing spawned Skye Fargo, ruthless, cold-blooded murder. Out of the acrid smoke of gunpowder still hanging in the air, he rose, cried out a promise never forgotten.

The Trailsman they began to call him all across the West: searcher, scout, hunter, the man who could see where others only looked, his skills for hire but not his soul, the man who lived each day to the fullest, yet trailed each tomorrow. Skye Fargo, the Trailsman, the seeker who could take the wildness of a land and the wanting of a woman and make them his own.

Virginia City, 1859—
Where the Good Book clears the path to
salvation, and the Book of Fargo provides the
means for survival.

1

Skye Fargo turned his lake-blue eyes toward Davidson Mountain, upon whose rocky side the mining town of Virginia City stuck precariously. The town wasn't much to look at, considering that it was one of the richest in the territory.

The preacher was standing beside Fargo. His name was Alfred Nelson, and he was a short, compact man who had worn nothing but black suits during their entire trek from Missouri. The suits hadn't traveled well, and the one he was wearing now was so thickly coated with alkali dust that it looked almost gray instead of black.

Nelson was a funny kind of a preacher, Fargo thought, because under the suit coat he wore a pistol that he knew how to use. He hadn't turned a hair on the trip out from Missouri when they'd passed the bones of animals—and sometimes of people—who'd come before and died on the way. He'd just spouted off some scripture about Ezekiel in the valley of dry bones, and wheels within wheels high up in the air. It didn't make a lot of sense to Fargo, but it seemed to mean something to the preacher. Now he was quoting scripture again.

"'A city that is set on a hill cannot be hid,'" Nelson said. "'Neither do men light a candle and put it under a bushel, but on a candlestick; and it gives light unto all that are in the house. Let your light so shine before men, that they may see your good works, and glorify your Father who is in heaven.' Book of Matthew, chapter five, verses fourteen through sixteen."

Fargo thought about Virginia City with all its whorehouses, opium dens, gambling halls, saloons, and billiard halls. He thought about the thieves, robbers, whores, gamblers, brawlers, and killers who were among the boomtown's inhabi-

1

tants. And he thought about the abandoned mine shafts with dead men lying at the bottom of them. Some of the men had fallen in when they were drunk or when the shafts had been covered with snow. A lot of the men hadn't fallen in by accident, however. Not unless they'd tied their hands and feet together first.

Fargo looked down at the little preacher and said, "The men up on that hill wouldn't know good works from Adam's off ox. Book of Fargo, chapter one."

The preacher kicked at the dirt, sending up a puff of dust.

"I don't believe I'm familiar with that book," he said.

"Wouldn't expect you to be," Fargo told him. "But it's the truth anyhow."

"Don't matter a bit to me whether it's the truth or not," Leo Harp said. "That's the place we've been looking for, so let's get ourselves on up there while it's still daylight."

The other men standing around them all muttered their agreement. They weren't a bad bunch, Fargo thought. They just didn't know what they were getting into.

Take Harp, for instance. He was a tall, wiry man who'd been a school teacher back in Missouri, or so he said, but he'd given up that profession to look for silver on a godforsaken mountain in the middle of nowhere. What kind of a chance did he have? Not much of one, in Fargo's estimation.

Nelson was different. The preacher wasn't planning to strike it rich or even work in the mines. His idea was to bring the word of the Lord to as rough a crew of men as there was anywhere in the West. He thought all he had to do was find a corner to stand on, bring out his Bible, and start preaching. If he did that, he was convinced that people would flock around him.

"They'll be hungry for the message of the Good Book," Nelson told Fargo early in their journey. "I'll have a crowd of a hundred before I say ten words."

Fargo thought he'd be lucky to have a crowd of ten by the time he'd said a million. Virginia City wasn't known for the spirituality of its citizens. They were too busy grubbing silver out of the guts of the mountain to do much praying. And if they weren't working, they were spending their money on things that were a lot closer to the works of Satan than to the works of God.

What Nelson believed or did wasn't any of Fargo's business, however, no more than it was his business what happened to any of them. There was Cal Edwards, a big bear of a man, who'd given up barbering for the lure of silver; Lane Utley, a tightly knit man burned brown from the sun, who'd been a farmer and decided he was tired of following a mule and a plow; Waymon Carter, who'd never worked a day in his life from what Fargo gathered, although he claimed to have been a justice of the peace; Jim Taylor, a shopkeeper, who'd been perhaps a bit more honest than the others and told Fargo that he was headed West to avoid the war that was sure to come.

"It'll tear Missouri apart," he said, "and I don't want to be here to see it. I'd just as soon go out West and get rich digging up the ground. The war will never get to Nevada Territory."

He was probably right about that, Fargo thought, but living in Virginia City was about as dangerous as being in a war. You were just as likely to get killed as if you were on the field of battle, except that like as not you'd never see your enemy, who'd probably back-shoot you or wait for you in an alley some dark night and knife you before you even knew he was there.

Fargo didn't think Taylor was afraid of danger, though. It was what would happen to his friends and neighbors that bothered him, and if he couldn't do anything about it, at least he didn't have to be a part of it.

"Well?" Harp said. "We've come all this way, what are we waiting for?"

Fargo was a trailsman, and he'd been hired to guide the men back in St. Jo. He'd gotten them to Nevada safely, across the plains and the great desert, and he'd done a good job of it. Hadn't lost a one of them. Now they were sitting on their horses there in the Carson Valley, and they could see their goal clinging to the mountain up high in the distance.

Fargo didn't blame them for being eager to get there, though he thought they'd all be better off if they gave up on any idea of striking it rich and just hired out to work in the mines. There was always a job there for a man with a strong back and a willingness to work down under the earth in the damp darkness of the treacherous tunnels.

For his part, Fargo would be glad to call an end to the journey, too. He'd taken half of his fee in advance, but the rest of it was due upon their arrival in Virginia City. He planned to keep it in his pocket and get out of Virginia City as soon as he could. There were more ways to lose your money—and more people who'd like to take it—in a town like that, than Fargo could count. And if Fargo knew anything about boomtowns, they'd invented a few more ways to take a man's money in just the last few days—or the last few hours.

"All right," he said, "let's get moving. We'll want to take it easy, though. By the time we pass through Gold Hill and get up to Virginia City, we'll be so high that we'll have to watch out for birds flying by our heads. Some people don't find it easy to breathe up there."

"We'll be fine," Harp said. "Come on."

He had always been the most impatient of the men, the first one to awaken in the mornings, urging everyone to get up and get started. Fargo had never minded. The quicker they got where they were going, the quicker he'd be paid.

He took the lead, and the men followed him, heading for their vision of El Dorado.

It was late afternoon when they reached the town, but they could hear the stamp mills pounding and the steam engines whistling. The noise never stopped in Virginia City. There were times during the day, and even during the night, when the earth shook and the buildings shivered because of underground explosions, but only newcomers were bothered. Everyone else had gotten used to it.

The town staggered up the mountain. Buildings that faced the street were propped up in back with high foundations or sometimes just stilts so flimsy that it seemed the blasting underneath would send them sliding down the mountainside, but that hadn't happened so far. There were still some people living in tents, though no one lived in caves or dugouts or coyote dens as some had in the earliest days of the town's great growth spurt.

Goats, the source of milk for the town, roamed the streets

4

along with stray dogs, miners, cardsharps, rounders of all kinds, and maybe even an honest citizen or two. There were wagons everywhere: wagons loaded with supplies going to the mines, wagons full of ore, wagons coming up from California with hard goods and food, including canned oysters and sardines. Nothing was too good for the rich citizens of Virginia City.

In Chinatown the houses and businesses crowded together so closely that no wagon could pass through the streets. The inhabitants didn't encourage visitors unless they were coming to do business in one of the many laundries.

On *D* street the whorehouses were ramshackle buildings that barely concealed what went on inside. The married women in town didn't like it, but the miners didn't care. They were hard men, and they liked their pleasure when they could get it.

The grandest structures in town were the saloons, though some of the mine owners had begun to build mansions to rival even those in San Francisco.

There were eight or nine hotels, but Fargo had no idea where his pilgrims were going to stay. Most of the hotel rooms would be taken by speculators, high-rolling gamblers, and men who had recently struck it rich.

However, like other things, where the men stayed after they got there was none of Fargo's business. He'd done what he was hired to do. Now his responsibilities were over.

They threaded their way through the crowded streets. No one paid them any mind. Everyone in Virginia City was used to strangers, and a few more didn't matter much one way or the other. Besides, in a boomtown, or any other town in the West for that matter, it was better not to pay much attention to strangers. Curiosity was likely to get you killed.

Fargo called them to a halt in front of the Iron Dog Saloon.

"All right," he said. "This is as far as I go. We'll all go inside and conduct our business, and after that you're on your own."

The preacher looked at the batwing doors. There was laughter coming from inside the saloon, and music, too. It wasn't church music, that was for sure.

"I don't think I much want to do business in a place like that," he said. "It looks like a den of thieves to me."

"No more than any other place in this town," Fargo said.

"He's right," Harp said.

It seemed he was always the one who spoke up first, Fargo thought. Maybe it had something to do with having been a teacher. No one seemed inclined to carry on the conversation, not even Nelson, so Fargo dismounted and looped the reins around the hitching post.

Fargo stepped up on the boardwalk and approached the batwings, when he saw that there was a large iron dog sitting beside them. It was painted black, but there were rust spots showing through the paint here and there.

"Good looking dog," Cal Edwards said, reaching over to pat it on the head. His huge hand covered the top of the head easily.

All the others, except Fargo and Nelson, patted the dog when Edwards was finished.

"Go ahead," Carter said to encourage them. "Might bring you good luck."

"I don't believe in luck," Nelson told him. "I believe in the Good Book."

"Not to mention that hogleg you have strapped on you," Taylor said.

"Never mind about that," Nelson said. "There's no conflict there. The Lord helps those who help themselves."

"What book of the Bible is that from?" Fargo asked.

"It's from a different book. One by a man named Poor Richard."

"You mean Benjamin Franklin?" Harp asked.

"One and the same. He had some wise things to say, even if he wasn't as good a Presbyterian as he should have been."

Lane Utley turned and spit tobacco into the street. He wiped his mouth on his sleeve and said, "Are we gonna stand out here talking until it gets dark, or are we gonna go in there and get our business done?"

"Come on," Nelson said, and pushed through the doors.

They were greeted by the sound of music from a badly out-of-tune piano. The air was thick with the smell of smoke, spilled beer, and cheap whiskey. There was a smoke cloud up around the high ceiling, and there was the sound of muttering talk coming from men sitting at the tables or standing at the bar. The gamblers didn't even look up when they walked in, and the saloon girls were all occupied with men who were pawing them or buying them drinks. Nobody cared that a group of strangers had just walked in.

Nobody, that is, except a tall woman in a feathery, flouncy dress that was tight at the waist and low at the top. She had red hair piled up on her head, and her high, full breasts pushed out over the neckline of her dress. She had a wide, generous mouth and clear green eyes. She was quite pretty, and Fargo wondered if she was new at her work. There was none of the hardness he would have expected to see in the face of a woman who'd worked in a saloon for more than a few months.

"Welcome, boys," she said. "I don't believe I've seen you in the Iron Dog before."

Nelson's face was as red as a hot brick. He opened his mouth to speak, but no words came out. Fargo wondered if he'd ever met a real sinner before.

"Our first time," Fargo said. "Looks like a mighty nice place."

He was just being polite, because the Iron Dog wasn't nice at all. It was hastily thrown together from whatever materials were available. The floor was rough, and the long mirror in back of the bar was cracked in two places. The piano music was about as bad as any Fargo had ever heard.

"Nothing but the best," the woman said. "My name's Marian."

"Fargo," the Trailsman said. "Skye Fargo."

The woman gave Fargo an appreciative look, taking in his tall body from head to boots.

"Any kin to the Wells-Fargoes?" she asked.

"Not as far as I know," Fargo said, though it wasn't strictly true. He had taken the name of his dead father's employer a good many years ago, so there was a connection between the names even if there was no relationship.

"Doesn't matter. Everybody's welcome in the Iron Dog. If you're here for the mining, I hope you all strike it rich. If you're not, well, enjoy your visit to the Iron Dog before you move along."

Marian turned and went to stand by the piano player, a little man dressed like the preacher. The piano itself was pock-marked with holes, and Fargo wondered what had caused them. He also wondered if Marian was going to sing, but she didn't seem inclined to. She was just positioning herself so that she could keep an eye on the room. Besides, thought Fargo, no one could sing in tune with that awful piano.

Fargo looked around the smokey room and saw a table in the back, near a wall. It looked like a good place for a private talk, and he started toward it, motioning for the others to follow him.

He sat down, and the other men pulled up chairs. Utley, Carter, Taylor, Edwards and Harp were all holding mugs of beer, having taken advantage of Marian's greeting to go to the bar for a drink. Harp had an extra mug for Fargo, and he handed it across the table.

Fargo took a swallow. It wasn't as bad as he'd expected, so he took another. Nelson watched them drink without any show of disapproval, but he clearly wished they'd get their business done so he could leave.

Fargo set his mug on the table and said, "Time to settle up. You all know what we agreed on."

"We do," Nelson said. "I've been holding the money."

He reached inside his suit coat and pulled out a leather pouch, shielding his movement from the rest of the room. He set the pouch on the table softly so that it wouldn't clink and advertise its contents. Then he pushed it across to Fargo, who took it in his big right hand and stuck it in his shirt just as surreptitiously as Nelson had removed it from its original hiding spot. It was all done so smoothly that no one in the room noticed what had happened, and that was the way Fargo wanted it.

"I'll buy you fellas a round," Fargo said. "And then it's time for you to do whatever it is you came here for."

"I appreciate the thought," Nelson said, "but I'll just go on my way now. I don't hold with drinking."

He stood up and reached across the table to shake Fargo's hand. He had a strong hand and a firm grip.

"May the good Lord be with you, Fargo," he said. "And all the rest of you."

"The Lord helps those that help themselves," Fargo "Book of Fargo."

Nelson grinned. "I see you've added a new verse. Or maybe I should say that you've stolen one."

"If you're going to steal, steal from the best," Fargo said. "And I reckon Ben Franklin was one of the best. Good luck to you, Preacher."

"Luck doesn't have a thing to do with it," Nelson said. "The Good Book does. Remember?"

"I remember," Fargo said, and Nelson left them with a wave and a smile.

"As for me," Utley said, "I'll take all the luck I can get. And I'll take that beer, too."

Everyone had a beer, and when they were finished, the men began drifting away, one by one. Utley left first, then Harp, then Edwards. Carter and Taylor stayed for another beer, then shook hands with Fargo and went out the batwing doors. Fargo thought he might as well be leaving, too. He'd have to find somewhere to spend the night, and the next morning he'd be on his way back down the mountain.

He was halfway to the doors when three men came through. They were big, bigger than Fargo, and two of them were swinging wooden clubs. The other one had a shotgun. They didn't look like men who'd come to have a peaceful drink, and Fargo suddenly wished he'd left a little earlier.

It might be turning into a long night.

2

The entrance of the three men got considerably more of a reaction than Fargo and his crew had only a short time before. The sound of the talk dropped in volume, then stopped, and after a few out-of-tune notes had tinkled from the piano, the music stopped, too.

The men with the clubs broke the silence by slapping the clubs into the palms of their hands.

"Well, well, well," the man with the shotgun said, looking around the room. "Looks like everybody here's having a real good time."

Nobody answered. Fargo stood where he was and looked over at Marian, who was standing by the piano. Her mouth was drawn into a tight line, and her face was as red as her hair.

"But you'd all be having a hell of a lot *more* fun," the man said, "if you was at the Gypsy Queen."

Fargo saw a movement out of the corner of his eye and turned his head slightly to the right, where he saw the bartender bending down behind the bar.

"Better not try that," the shotgunner called out to him as the men at the bar cleared a space in front of the bartender. "I'd hate to ruin what's left of that old mirror you got in here."

The bartender stood up and showed that his hands were empty.

"That's better. Now then, why don't we all move on out and go on over to the Gypsy Queen, where there's a real good time for everybody."

He and his two companions stepped to the side as if clearing the way for everyone to leave, but no one got up.

The man cocked the shotgun, pulling the hammers back

with his thumb. The clicking noise was loud in the quiet saloon.

"Maybe you all didn't hear me," he said. "So I'll just say it again. It's time to leave this place and get to a better one."

"That's right, Slade," Marian said. "You take everybody right on over to the Gypsy Queen, where the drinks are all watered, and the girls are all poxy."

Slade rounded on her. He was hatchet-faced, with a slit for a mouth, narrow eyes, and a flat nose.

"Now, Marian, I wish you hadn't said that. You know how it hurts Esmeralda's feelings when somebody talks bad about her place."

"That's too bad. If her place was any good, and if she didn't cheat everybody who walks through the doors, she wouldn't have to send a man with a shotgun over here to persuade people to pay it a visit."

Slade looked at the two men with the clubs and shook his head sadly.

"It's too bad, the way a woman has to talk so much and spoil things. We were just about to take care of business without any damages, and now I guess I'll just have to shoot something. How about the piano?"

"Go ahead," Marian said. "It's never recovered from your last visit here. Why don't you just put it out of its misery."

Well, Fargo thought, *now I know why the piano sounds so bad.*

While the conversation was going on, Fargo had been moving imperceptibly, getting himself closer to Slade. He didn't like to mix in other folks' trouble, but at the same time, he didn't like to see an unarmed woman being bullied by a man with a shotgun. For that matter, he didn't like to see anybody get bullied. It just didn't seem right, somehow.

"If that's what you want," Slade said, "I'll take care of it for you."

He put the stock of the shotgun to his shoulder and took aim at the piano. The piano player scooted off his bench, nearly falling down in his hurry to get out of the way. Marian stood where she was, unmoving.

"You can get out of the way if you want to," Slade told her. "That thing's likely to come apart like the one-hoss shay."

"I don't think so," Fargo said, being close enough to Slade now to do something about him.

Slade started to turn to see who was talking to him, and Fargo helped him out. He grabbed Slade's shoulder and spun him, knocking the shotgun barrel up and away with his left arm and slamming his right fist into the center of Slade's solar plexus. The fist traveled only about ten inches, but it struck like a wooden mallet. Slade's eyes widened in pain as his breath left him. He dropped the shotgun, and the Trailsman caught it before it hit the floor.

Fargo straightened, holding the shotgun steady on the other two men. They had finally figured out what was going on, and their clubs were poised to slam into Fargo's head.

"Uh-uh," Fargo said. He shook his head. "You two boys just put those things down on the floor and help your Mr. Slade there."

Slade was on his knees, his hands clutched to his chest. He was gasping for breath, and his face was the color of a tomato.

"He might have a couple of broken ribs," Fargo said, "so you'll want to be gentle with him when you're helping him get up."

The two men looked at Fargo, then at Slade, then back at Fargo, who waggled the shotgun barrel.

"Better do what I said," Fargo told them. "Else I'm going to have to pull this trigger."

The men tossed the clubs on the floor. They clattered and bounced.

"That's better," Fargo said. "Now you can see to your friend."

They went to Slade, who still couldn't quite catch his breath. He looked at Fargo with hatred burning in his narrow eyes as the two men helped him to his feet.

"Better get on out of here before I decide to shoot you the way you were going to shoot the piano," Fargo said. "You can go on back to that Gypsy Queen you're so fond of."

The men started out of the saloon. Slade was moving slowly, shuffling his feet as if he were a very old man.

When they had passed out through the batwings, Fargo walked over to the bar and laid the shotgun on it.

"Take care of this," he told the bartender. "Put it under

there with the one you already have. Maybe next time you'll be ready when those fellas come in."

While he was speaking, the piano started to play again, an off-key rendition of "Oh, Susannah," and the talking resumed at the tables and at the bar. Men moved to fill in the space around Fargo, and one of them offered to buy him a drink.

"Better not," Fargo said. "I have to find me a place to stay tonight."

"Maybe I could help you there," Marian said at his back. "Come on over to my table, and I'll buy you a whiskey."

Fargo looked at the man next to him, who winked. Fargo turned to Marian.

"Now that's an invitation I can't refuse," he said. "Show me that table. And a beer would be fine."

Marian led him to a vacant table in the back of the room near a staircase leading up to the second floor. There wasn't much doubt that some of the saloon girls did a little business up there, Fargo thought.

Marian stood at the table looking at Fargo, and for a second he didn't know what she wanted. Then he figured it out and pulled out a chair for her, holding it until she sat down, then scooting it up to the table. He sat across from her just as the bartender arrived with a glass of beer and set it on the table.

"I don't believe I ever saw a man who could hit as hard as you," Marian said, as Fargo took a drink of beer.

"I figured he needed a lesson," Fargo said.

"You were right about that. And so does Esmeralda. She's been trying to run me out of business ever since I came to town. This isn't the first time Slade's paid me a visit."

"So I figured," Fargo said, looking at the piano.

Marian laughed. "I know it sounds awful, but I can't buy another one. It cost me more than I could afford to get that one here."

"Virginia City has police," Fargo said. "You could call them."

"Esmeralda has them in her pocket. They're all on her pay-roll."

"You could pay them more."

"No, I couldn't." Marian paused. "Or maybe I could. But I don't believe in paying off people who're supposed to be

13

working for me already. Anyway, they have a lot more to worry about than my little problems. There are people being killed on the streets every day, and the stage is robbed every other day. So why would the police concern themselves with me? What I want to do is hire someone to help me out."

Fargo took a swallow of beer and set the glass on the table.

"You mean me," he said.

"That's right. You can handle yourself, and you're not afraid of Slade like all the other men in this place. They're not afraid to go down under the ground in mines that might cave in on them or blow up or catch fire, but you saw what happened when Slade came in. Nobody stood up to him, except you. They like my liquor, and they like my girls, but they don't want to pick a fight with Slade."

"They probably know him better than I do."

"They do. I won't lie to you about Slade. He's a dangerous man, and a bad man to have for an enemy." She looked at Fargo, who was calmly drinking the last of his beer. "Though you don't seem bothered by that idea."

Fargo thought about his situation. He didn't need money, not with what he'd just been paid. But he didn't have any particular place to go, and he did need a place to spend the night. And he thought from Marian's tone that her offer of a job might include a few things that she hadn't mentioned yet, things that he might enjoy more than money.

"Well?" Marian said. "Do you want the job or not?"

"I'd need a place to stay," Fargo said.

Marian smiled. "I think that can be arranged. I have a few rooms here if you don't mind staying in a saloon."

"Would I get any sleep?"

"The noise dies down after a while. And besides, you don't look like a man who'd let a little noise bother him."

Fargo looked into her emerald eyes.

"I wasn't thinking about noise," he said.

Marian's gaze didn't waver.

"There might be something that would keep you awake for a while. But you'd just sleep all the better for it later on."

"Sounds good to me," Fargo said, and gave her a grin. "When do I start?"

"You already have," Marian told him.

14

Fargo looked around the little room to which Marian had directed him. It was furnished with a bed, a washstand, and a straight-backed wooden chair. A pitcher and a cracked bowl sat on the washstand. A window with gauzy curtains looked out over the street.

It wasn't much of a room, Fargo thought, but then he didn't need much in the way of comforts, and it would suit him just fine. It wasn't as if he was planning to live there permanently.

He had stabled his big Ovaro stallion in a livery not far from the saloon, and Marian had agreed to pay the owner as part of Fargo's fee.

Fargo was glad to be getting his own room as part of the fee as well. Lodging in Virginia City was around four dollars a night, a price that Fargo considered far too high. After all, most of the miners were paid no more than five dollars a day, which was what Marian had offered Fargo. Not bad, he thought, with a free room and other benefits.

He was thinking of what those other benefits might be when there was a light tapping on the door of his room.

"Come on in," Fargo said. "It's not locked."

In fact, it couldn't be locked, as he had discovered earlier. If the room was used by the saloon girls for business, Marian wouldn't want them to be able to lock themselves in. There were good reasons for that. Sometimes customers got rough, and the girls needed a quick getaway. Also, Marian wouldn't want them striking any private deals with the men they were entertaining, and the insecure doors would discourage that sort of thing.

Marian came into the room. She was still wearing the dress she'd worn downstairs, and she brushed a feather away from her face as she looked around.

"Does it suit you?" she asked.

"It's fine," Fargo said. "I've slept in a lot worse places. Have a seat."

"Thank you," Marian said, and sat in the only chair. "You're not regretting having taken a job with me, are you?"

"Not yet," Fargo said, "but I'm not exactly sure what I've let myself in for."

Marian shifted in the chair and crossed her legs. In doing so she pulled up her dress and made no attempt to conceal anything. Fargo admired her slim calves and sweet plump knees. She didn't seem to mind.

"I'll tell you what you're in for," she said. "There are twenty-five saloons in this town, give or take one or two, but mine's the biggest and the best."

Fargo didn't doubt it.

"There's just one problem," Marian continued.

"The Gypsy Queen," Fargo said.

"That's right. Esmeralda, the owner, is no more a gypsy than I am. She's from somewhere back East, but she has olive skin and dark hair, so she passes herself off as a gypsy. She thinks it makes her seem mysterious. But that doesn't matter. What matters is that she's jealous of me."

Fargo gave her knees another glance and said that he didn't much blame Esmeralda.

"I'm not talking about that kind of jealousy. She jealous of my business. Of those twenty-five saloons I told you about, only two of them are owned by women. She thinks that only one of them should be."

"Why's that?"

"Jealousy, pure and simple. She was here first, by about a month. Then I came in, and I took a good part of her business away because I don't water the whiskey, and nobody here cheats at cards. And all my girls are clean, which is something you can't say about the girls at Esmeralda's."

"You mentioned something about the girls at her place to Slade," Fargo said.

"I run a clean place," Marian said. "But this isn't a whorehouse."

"I never thought it was."

"But of course I have some working girls. A saloon has to have a few women around to brighten things up. Men like a place better if there's somebody to flatter them and make them feel good."

"Women like that kind of thing, too," Fargo said.

Marian smiled. "That's true. So why don't you flatter me?"

"I was thinking about it, but you seemed to want to talk business."

"I figure we've pretty much settled our business dealings, don't you?"

Fargo gave her a slow smile.

"I'd say that was pretty much up to you."

"I knew when I saw you come in that you were going to be trouble," Marian said.

"Trouble?"

"You know what kind of trouble I mean."

"I guess maybe I do, at that," Fargo said.

"Then come over here and help me get out of this dress," Marian told him.

3

It didn't take long to get Marian undressed. It was as easy as peeling a hard-boiled egg, and for that matter she hadn't needed much help, if any. She'd just asked Fargo to help for the fun of it. She slid out of the dress and her undergarments like an eel. She was tall, and it was immediately obvious that she was a natural redhead. Her breasts stood high and proud, tipped with ruby nipples that stiffened as Fargo looked at her with admiration.

Something else was stiffening, too, and Fargo got out of his own clothes while he could still do so with some grace.

"Not bad," Marian said, looking him over from top to bottom. "Some big men just look big with their clothes on and are pretty small when they get them off. But not you."

"Glad you're not disappointed," Fargo said.

Marian put her hands on her amply curved hips and said, "What about you?"

"Am I disappointed, you mean? No, ma'am, not by a long shot."

Marian stepped boldly over to him until the tip of his rigid rod was touching her flat stomach just above her curly reddish-gold pubic hair. Then she took a moment to look into his eyes before taking one more step.

Her breasts flattened against Fargo's chest, her nipples hot as a Texas branding iron in springtime. He could feel the heat coming off her lower body as well. His erection was lying along her hot, flat stomach, which she pressed against him, causing the erection to twitch involuntarily.

"Umm," she said. "That feels good."

Fargo reached behind her and cupped the cheeks of her buttocks with his hands, pulling her even closer. There wasn't room to slip a playing card between them.

"I wouldn't want you to get the wrong idea about this," Marian said, her voice a throaty whisper.

"I don't think I am," Fargo told her, massaging the two mounds of flesh that he held.

"I mean, I don't want you to feel obligated to me just because I'm your boss. If you don't want to go any further, just say the word."

"I don't know what the word is," Fargo told her. "But whatever it is, I won't be saying it."

He rubbed against her, letting her feel the hardness that was trapped between them.

"Ahhhh," Marian said. "Yes, I don't believe you will."

She kissed him then, opening her mouth and taking in his tongue, meeting it with her own. They stood that way for a few seconds. When they broke apart, Marian moved away a step. She reached down and took hold of Fargo's throbbing member.

"Quite a handful," she said, giving it a gentle tug.

For an answer Fargo removed his hands from her ass and put them on her generous breasts, feeling the hot, hard tips burn against his palms.

"More than a handful," he said, pushing her slowly backward to the bed.

She fell across it, her legs open and ready.

Fargo reached for her dress, which was lying on the chair nearby. He felt one of the feathers, and he pulled it loose.

"What's that for?" Marian asked, propping herself up on her elbows and eyeing the feather suspiciously.

Fargo didn't answer. Instead, he turned the feather sideways and ran it up her slit, letting it tickle her moistened mound.

Marian closed her eyes and shuddered with pleasure. Fargo drew the feather upward again, and she collapsed on the bed, letting her legs open even wider. Fargo tickled her with the tip of the feather, then withdrew it, then touched her again. He did it several times, until her legs were twitching and she was practically bouncing on the bed.

"I want you in me, Fargo," she said. "Now! All of you! Hurry!"

Fargo didn't need any further urging. Her excited delight had practically turned his pole to iron. He stepped to the bed, lowered himself, and plunged inside her.

There was no resistance. She was so hot and slick and wet that he went straight in, right up to the root. He was ready to begin thrusting, but Marian threw her arms around him and clasped him with her legs, holding him in place. He could feel the muscles in her vagina clasping and unclasping on him, and though he would have said it was impossible, his erection continued to grow even larger.

Still holding him in place, Marian began to rotate her hips beneath him. If she kept that up much longer, Fargo thought, he wasn't going to be able to hold back.

Marian loosened her hold at that moment, and Fargo withdrew slowly. Then he went back inside her, just as slowly, all the way. Marian urged him to go faster, but Fargo took his time, enjoying each sensation. Judging by Marian's gasps, she was enjoying it as well. But after a few seconds, Fargo couldn't resist any longer, and his thrusts became shorter and quicker.

"Yes!" Marian said. "Give it to me! Just like that! Just like that!"

Fargo gave it to her, and just when he thought that he couldn't last any longer, she said, "Now, Fargo! Oh God. Oh God! Oh! Oh!"

She clawed at his back and thrashed beneath him as if she were having some kind of spasm, and Fargo jetted hot streams of himself into her, one after another.

Marian subsided under him at last and was still. After a while she said, "You're even more of a man than I thought, Skye Fargo."

Fargo moved to lie beside her. He said, "And you're much more of a woman, Marian. I think I'm going to like working here."

"It's not all going to be this much fun," Marian said.

"Are you sure?"

"I wish I wasn't," she said, "but you'll find out."

And it wasn't long before he did.

*   *   *

20

The trouble started two nights later with a gambler named Williams, who wore a black frock coat, a white shirt and tie, and a fancy hat. He took the hat off when he played and put it under his chair. He had long gray hair that was getting a little thin on top and a neatly trimmed moustache the same color gray as his hair. His watery blue eyes didn't miss a thing that went on at the table where he played.

It was easy to see that he'd been around for a while. He knew his way around a saloon, and he was a good cardplayer. Fargo didn't doubt that. But it seemed that he was winning a lot more often than he should, especially when he had the deal, and it wasn't long before people started to complain.

"I don't give a damn what they say," Williams told Fargo when he was confronted. He had to speak up to be heard over the sound of the tinny, out-of-tune piano. "I'm not cheating, and they know it. They're just mad because they're losing. Now let me get back to the game."

Fargo let him go. He didn't trust the man, mainly because Williams was winning nearly every single time he dealt. When others were dealing, his luck wasn't nearly as good, though he was holding his own even then.

But if there was cheating going on, Fargo couldn't figure out how Williams could be doing it. Fargo checked the cards more than once and found nothing wrong. He even brought out a fresh deck, but that didn't change anything. Williams kept right on winning, especially when he was dealing.

It took Fargo several hours of close watching, but he finally thought he knew what was happening. Williams had a big mug of black coffee beside him, sitting well back from the edge of the table. Williams said he never drank anything stronger because liquor dulled his senses and threw off his game, but Fargo noticed that he never drank any of the coffee, either. It just sat there in the mug, its dark, flat surface still as a mirror.

And in fact, that was what it was: a mirror. When Williams dealt, he could see the cards reflected in the coffee. He might not be able to see all of them, but he could probably see enough to give him quite an edge. And when he was dealing the players cards to replace those they tossed away, he went much slower and could see much better.

Fargo was about to call him on it, but he was too late. One

of the players who had been losing steadily couldn't stand it any longer. He was a big miner, with skin pale as a fish belly because he spent all his daylight hours under the ground. He wasn't pale now, however. His face was a fiery red, and his eyes were narrow with anger. He stood up, kicked his chair backward, and said, "You son of a bitch. You've cheated me for the last time."

He reached across the table and grabbed Williams by the front of his white shirt and pulled him out of his chair.

"I'm gonna beat you within an inch of your life," the miner said.

Williams didn't reply. He just calmly reached inside his coat, pulled out a little one-shot pistol about the size of a watch fob, and shot the miner right in the bridge of the nose.

The pistol made hardly any noise at all, and the bullet was of such a small caliber that the miner didn't know he was dead for a second or two. He stood there looking at Williams, his eyes wide with surprise. He released his grip on Williams's shirt to brush at his face as if he'd been bitten by a mosquito.

Williams slumped back into his chair, quickly hiding the little gun back inside his coat.

The miner waved his hand in front of his eyes, but he wasn't seeing anything. He reached behind him, and his hand touched the back of his chair. He leaned his weight on it, but the chair scooted backward. The miner fell heavily, and dust puffed up around him when he hit the rough wooden floor.

Up until that point everyone in the saloon had been frozen as stiff as icicles and just as quiet. But when the miner hit the floor, all hell broke loose.

Two of the other miners who'd been gambling at the table jumped across it and grabbed for Williams. The table collapsed under them, and they landed in a tangle on top of it. Williams was out of his chair and running for the back door of the saloon before they could get to their feet.

The piano player, a short, skinny man named Glenn, stuck out a sticklike leg and tripped Williams. Before he hit the floor, there were two men on him, beating him with their fists while a third stood beside them, kicking Williams in the ribs.

Fargo tried to get to Williams before the gambler was killed. One man was already dead, and that was bad enough.

Fargo was determined not to let the number increase. It wasn't that he cared so much about Williams. It was just that murders weren't exactly good for business. People got killed in Virginia City every day, but Marian liked to brag that nothing like that went on in her place of business. It did now, though, and Fargo wanted to make sure things didn't get even worse.

Three big miners stepped in front of Fargo as he started toward Williams. He pushed the one in the middle aside and walked between the others. He didn't get far. One of them put an oak-hard forearm around his neck and jerked him backward while the miner who'd been pushed out of the way waded in with both fists swinging.

Fargo tried to ignore the fact that he could hardly breathe. He reached behind the man who held him and locked his hands together. When he was sure he was braced, he jumped up and kicked the miner who was hitting him. His right boot heel took the man in the face and straightened him up. With his left foot, Fargo kicked him squarely between the legs.

The man staggered backward, gagging, his face purple.

The miner who was holding Fargo squeezed tighter, completely cutting off Fargo's air supply, while the third man took the first one's place. He was faster and trickier, and he got in a couple of quick blows to Fargo's midsection before jumping back. He wasn't going to let Fargo kick him.

So instead Fargo stomped as hard as he could on the instep of the man who had him by the neck.

The man let go immediately, reaching for his foot. Fargo turned so fast that he was just a blur and clapped his cupped hands on the man's ears.

The man screamed, and Fargo hoped he'd broken his eardrums. He whirled on the third man, who was poised to land a kidney punch. The man was surprised when Fargo turned so quickly, and even more surprised when Marian hit him over the head with a whiskey bottle.

Two men grabbed Marian, and three more grabbed Fargo and dragged him down. He was pretty sure he wasn't going to be able to get up, but then he heard the boom of a shotgun. It was about time Ray, the bartender, remembered what the shotgun was for, Fargo thought.

The men that had been holding Fargo down got up and

melted away into the crowd. Fargo stood and looked for Marian. She wasn't far away. No one was near her.

Fargo nodded to her and started throwing people out of his way as he went to where Williams lay face down on the floor. The gambler wasn't moving, and there was a line of blood on the wood beside his mouth. His face was already beginning to swell and change color from the bruises.

The fact that it was changing color was a good sign, Fargo thought. It meant that Williams wasn't dead. Not yet, anyway.

Fargo looked over at Glenn. The skinny piano player was sitting on his stool, looking as if he wished he were somewhere else. California, maybe.

"Let's have some music," Fargo said.

Glenn turned to the piano and started playing a sad rendition of "Sweet Betsy from Pike." Of course anything would have sounded sad on that piano.

"Drinks for everybody," Marian said. "Except those who can't walk."

She was referring to the miner Fargo had kicked. He was sitting on the floor, clutching himself. And of course Williams wouldn't be drinking anything, either, much less walking.

"I'll talk to Ray about sending for the police," Marian said, as the crowd headed for the bar. She looked at Williams. "We need to talk to him before they get here."

"I'll take him to my room," Fargo said, slipping his hands under Williams and lifting him. "I hope Ray's serving the cheap stuff to this bunch."

"He'd better," Marian said.

Fargo threw Williams on the bed. The gambler stirred, and his eyelids fluttered, but he didn't wake up.

"Here," Marian said, coming into the room and handing Fargo a bottle of whiskey. "Give him some of this."

Fargo uncorked the bottle and lifted the gambler's head. Williams's lips were slightly parted, so Fargo poured some liquor into his mouth.

Williams swallowed, sputtered, and shook his head. His body jerked, and he sat up. He didn't say anything. He just sat there, staring blankly around the room.

"Give him some more," Marian said, and Fargo tilted

Williams's head back and poured some more whiskey down him.

This time Williams did more than sputter. He coughed and twitched and finally said, "What the hell happened?"

"You killed a man," Fargo said, "and then you got the crap kicked out of you. You're lucky you aren't dead yourself." Fargo looked at Marian's face. "Or maybe you aren't so lucky."

"Let me talk to him," Marian said, her voice tight.

Fargo stepped aside. Williams reached for the bottle that Fargo was holding, but the Trailsman pulled it out of his reach.

"Who sent you here?" Marian asked.

"I need a drink," Williams said.

"Talk first. Then you can have something."

Williams shook his head. "I didn't mean to kill that man. It was self-defense. Everybody saw it."

"I don't care about that one way or the other," Marian said. "I want to know who sent you here."

Williams looked longingly at the bottle Fargo was holding. It was obvious that he did like something stronger than coffee now and then. Fargo smiled at him.

"Tell her what she wants to know," he said.

"Nobody sent me. I'm a gambler, and I heard the Iron Dog was a place that played square. That's why I came."

"You weren't playing square," Fargo said. "You were cheating those miners. I don't blame them for being mad."

"That's a lie. I wasn't cheating. I don't have to cheat to beat them. I'm just too good for them, and they don't want to admit it."

Marian reached out and slapped his face. The sharp sound of flesh on flesh echoed in the small room. Williams's head snapped to the side. He didn't turn it back.

"If Fargo says you were cheating, you were cheating," Marian said. "I'm going to ask you one more time. Who sent you here?"

Williams sat there with his head hanging over to one side and said nothing.

"All right, then," Marian said. "Kill him, Fargo."

Fargo had no intention of killing anybody, but he was willing to play along with Marian's little game.

"Yes, ma'am," he said.

Williams turned his head to watch as Fargo drew the big Colt from its holster.

"Sorry I have to do this," Fargo said, thumbing back the hammer.

Williams flinched and put up a hand, as if that would stop a bullet.

"No," he said. "You can't."

Fargo let the hammer back down.

"You're right. I can't. Too much noise. Half the people in the saloon would figure out what happened, those that are sober enough to do any figuring."

He holstered the Colt, and a look of relief crossed Williams's face. But the look changed to one of horror as Fargo bent and retrieved the Arkansas toothpick from his boot.

"This'll be a lot quieter," Fargo said. He looked at Marian. "Be a little bit messier, though. People bleed as bad as a hog."

"I don't care," Marian said. "I'll have the sheets changed."

"For God's sake!" Williams said.

"I don't think God has a whole lot to do with this," Fargo told him, testing the edge of the knife with the ball of his thumb.

He stepped to the bed so fast that Williams didn't have time to react. He grabbed Williams by the hair and jerked back his head, exposing the gambler's throat. He put the blade of the knife right above Williams's adam's apple, and a thin red line of blood popped out on the skin.

"Jesus!" Williams said. "Don't! It was Esmeralda, goddamn her! She paid me fifty dollars to come here and take the money from those miners. She said to cheat them any way I could."

Once he got started talking, he didn't seem to want to stop.

"She told me that nothing would happen. She said she'd make everything right."

"I don't see her around here coming to help you out any," Fargo said, sliding the blade just the tiniest bit and letting a little more blood flow from the gambler's neck. "Do you?"

"No. She lied to me. She knew I'd get caught. I can see now that was her plan all along."

"I think he's telling the truth," Fargo said. "You want me to kill him anyway?"

"Might as well," Marian said. "He's no use to us now."

4

Williams fainted. Fargo didn't remember ever having seen a man faint before. He let Williams flop back on the bed and wiped his knife blade on the gambler's black coat.

"I think we scared him," Fargo said.

"I'd say so," Marian said, smiling. "The son of a bitch deserved it. For that matter, he deserved killing."

"Maybe," Fargo said, "but that's something for the law to decide."

Marian met his eyes. "I know that. I didn't really mean for you to kill him. I was planning to turn him over to the law all along. I just wanted you to scare him some. And you did a good job of it. Now we know why he was here."

"Better than a man with a shotgun," Fargo said.

"I'm not so sure. This is going to cause plenty of trouble. I told you that Esmeralda was paying off the police. They'll make this into something more than it is."

"No they won't," Fargo told her. "We have a dead man, and we have his killer. That's all there is to it."

"We'll see," Marian said.

It took a while to get things sorted out, but they turned out pretty much as Fargo had predicted. Williams was hauled off to jail, and the police seemed to be satisfied, all except for a big lunk with a face that appeared to have been carved right out of the side of Davidson Mountain. He was a deputy marshal named Sullivan, and he wasn't happy at all. His craggy face was red, and his small piggy eyes were hard and black as coal.

"I think you're lyin', old son," he told Fargo. "I think this man here is as innocent as a newborn babe, and he has the marks of your beatin' on him to prove it."

What Fargo thought was proved was that while Esmeralda might not be able to buy the whole police force, she might be able to buy a piece or two of it, and Sullivan was one of the pieces she'd bought.

Sullivan was overruled, however, and Williams was taken away. Later that night in Fargo's room, Marian said, "He'll be out of jail by now and on his way to San Francisco."

"You can't be sure of that," Fargo said. "They might keep him for a while."

"That shows how much you know about the way things work here. Esmeralda will have her way. You'll see."

"I'd like to meet this Esmeralda," Fargo said.

"No you wouldn't. She's trouble, Fargo."

"What about you?"

"Me? What kind of trouble could I be?"

Fargo touched her naked body in a certain place.

"This kind," he said. He touched her again. "Or that kind."

Marian shuddered and sighed. Then she said, "Now that's the kind of trouble I understand."

Fargo hoped it was all the trouble he'd have in Virginia City, but two days later, he found out different when Sullivan and two other men came to the Iron Dog and arrested him for murder.

Fargo thought about resisting, but not for long. He could see it was no use. They had come in the middle of the afternoon, during one of the rare lulls in the saloon's business, and caught everyone off guard. Ray didn't even think about going for the shotgun. Sullivan or one of the others would have killed him before he got it and justified it by saying he was interfering with their arrest. And of course they would have been right. Fargo didn't want anyone to get hurt, so he went peacefully. Marian promised she'd have him out before dark, but Fargo had his doubts. He wasn't sure Sullivan would ever let him out, not if he had any say in the matter.

The Virginia City jail was bigger than Fargo had thought it would be, but then he should have known that it would be sizeable. There was more than enough crime in a mining town to fill up two or three jails.

Sullivan and the men put Fargo in a cell that for some reason was located in its own area, separate from the others. Fargo thought he knew what the reason was. This would be a cell where prisoners could be dealt with in any way Sullivan or someone else wanted to deal with them, and there would be no witnesses.

Wouldn't want to scare the other prisoners, Fargo thought. At least not too much.

Sullivan handed one of the other men his pistol. The man took it, and he and the other one left, locking the door behind them. Fargo watched them go, conscious of Sullivan standing across from him, smiling.

"Mr. Fargo, is it?" Sullivan asked.

"That's my name," Fargo said.

"A mighty fancy-lookin' fella you are, too, I must say. Well, you won't be fancy-lookin' for long. I wonder if Miss Marian will still like you when I'm done."

"Why?" Fargo said.

It was only a single word, but Sullivan knew exactly what he meant.

"Because you're standin' in the way of progress, my friend. That's all it is, a simple business proposition. Miss Esmeralda wants more business, and she needs to get Miss Marian's customers. You're preventin' that. So that's the reason for the beatin' you'll take. Call it a lesson, if you will. As for the other, well, I can't really say, except that you shouldn't have killed your friend."

Fargo was puzzled by the last remark.

"Friend?" Fargo said. "I didn't kill anybody, much less my friend."

"Oh, but you did. His name was Taylor, I believe, Jim Taylor. Don't tell me you didn't know him."

Fargo was surprised to hear of Taylor's death, but he knew he wasn't to blame for it.

"I know him," he said. "He was in a party I guided out here, but I haven't seen him since I got to town."

Sullivan smiled, revealing a mouthful of large white teeth.

"Ah, but that's a good story," he said, "and you should keep right on tellin' it. Maybe you'll find someone to believe you. Not me, of course, but someone of less intelligence and low cunning." He paused. "But while it's been very pleasant to pass the time of day with you, I'm afraid that now it's time for the lesson. After all, you might accidentally get out of here, and we want you to know just how things stand."

"I don't guess it would do any good to tell you that I understand how things stand already."

"Sure, and that's a fine idea, but I'm afraid my employer wouldn't approve if I let you off so easy."

With no further warning, Sullivan moved in on Fargo, hitting him with a quick right and left in the stomach. His fists were as hard as ribbed iron and Fargo stumbled back, the backs of his knees striking the bunk. He fell onto the bed and Sullivan hit him in the face twice before Fargo could even get his hands up.

Sullivan surprised Fargo. He moved back, dancing lightly on his toes. He wasn't even breathing heavily.

"I was hoping you'd give me more of a fight, Fargo," he said. "You're big enough, and I hear you're handy with your fists. You don't seem too handy to me. Why don't you show me something?"

Fargo got off the bed, but Sullivan was fast. Very fast. He hit Fargo low, and then he hit him high. Fargo lurched backward. Sullivan followed closely, hitting him with short, hard jabs. Fargo had never fought a man like Sullivan before, one who seemed to know exactly what he was doing. What he was doing was giving Fargo a thorough beating.

There was no way to fight him fairly, not now that Sullivan had the advantage. He was like a machine, his arms pumping, his fists hitting, one-two, one-two.

So Fargo decided to fight unfairly. They'd taken away his Colt when they arrested him, but they weren't very good at their jobs. They hadn't even looked at his boots.

Fargo went down, pretending to be hurt much worse than he was. He lay there in a crumpled heap breathing heavily while Sullivan toe-danced above him.

"Not so tough, after all," Sullivan said. "Sure, and I've fought a few nancy-boys who had more gumption than you, Fargo. Get up off the floor, and be a man."

Fargo didn't move. He even stopped breathing.

"Ah, but it's no good, my boy," Sullivan said. "I can see that you're as alive as ever you were. Get up, and try to show me something."

Fargo lay there, unmoving, and after a few more seconds Sullivan couldn't stand it any longer. He stopped his little dance and leaned down, reaching as if to put a thumb in Fargo's eye to wake him.

Fargo struck like a rattler. He brought the knife out of his boot and stuck the point of it right in the soft spot under Sullivan's chin. Sullivan's mouth was closed, and it stayed that way as Fargo stood up, rising to his full height and bringing Sullivan right up with him.

"It wouldn't take much," Fargo said. "Just one quick push and this blade would run through your mouth and tongue and straight to your brain. If you have one that is."

Sullivan's little eyes glared hate, but he wisely didn't try to talk.

"Now here's what we're going to do," Fargo said, holding the knife so that it bit into Sullivan's chin. "We're going to talk things over like two intelligent men of low cunning. I didn't kill Jim Taylor. I didn't even know he was dead. But now I'm curious. I want to know two things. The first is how Taylor died, and the second is who sent you to me."

It had occurred to Fargo while Sullivan was having his fun that very few people in Virginia City knew there was any connection between Fargo and Taylor. So who would have accused Fargo of the murder? That was something Fargo really wanted to find out.

"I'm going to relax just a little," Fargo told Sullivan. "Enough for you to talk. But if you try anything, I doubt you'll be much for conversation. Understand?"

Fargo relaxed just enough to let Sullivan nod.

"Good. Now tell me how Taylor died."

"Bushwhacked. Outside of town. Somebody found the body and brought him in."

"I haven't been outside of town since I got here," Fargo said. "Anybody who works at the Iron Dog could have told you that if you'd just asked. Who was it that tied me into it?"

"I don't know that," Sullivan said through gritted teeth.

Fargo thought that over. Maybe Sullivan was telling the truth, but it didn't seem likely. Fargo would have bet good money that Sullivan had made the arrest without any authority behind him.

"I think you do know," Fargo said. "I think you decided to arrest me yourself because you knew Esmeralda would approve."

"Now that's where you'd be wrong," Sullivan said. "I did it because you're a filthy murderin' bastard."

Fargo decided it didn't matter who'd told Sullivan, at least not right now. What he wanted to do was get out of the cell before Sullivan tried something. Fargo didn't like Sullivan, but he didn't want to have to kill him.

"All right," Fargo said. "Have it your way. But I didn't murder anyone, and I have plenty of witnesses who'll swear I haven't left town. I can get them for you any time you want them. Can you bring yours?"

Sullivan said nothing.

"I didn't think so. Now here's what we'll do. You go take hold of the bars in the door with both hands, and I'll take this knife away from your throat. Then I'll just stick it in the back of your neck while you call your two friends to come let us out of here."

Sullivan looked for a second as if he might rather die, but he finally gave an almost imperceptible nod. They went over to the cell door, and when Sullivan gripped the bars, Fargo moved the knife, but so quickly that Sullivan didn't have a chance to try anything.

"When you call them," Fargo said, "tell them to bring my pistol."

"They won't do that," Sullivan said.

"They will if you put it to them right." Fargo jabbed the point of his knife into the skin at the back of Sullivan's neck, drawing blood. "Why don't you try it and see."

"Barlow!" Sullivan called. "Butler! Get your sorry asses in here. And bring Fargo's gun with you. He might want to use it to shoot himself."

Fargo wondered how many men in that cell had shot themselves, or to put it the way it really was, how many had been shot by Sullivan.

Butler and Barlow came into the hallway laughing, but they stopped when they saw Sullivan pressed up against the bars.

"First thing you do," Fargo said, "is take your pistols and lay them on the floor. Mine, too. And do it real slow."

The two men looked at each other and then at Sullivan, who said, "Do what he tells you, goddamnit!"

They thought it over and then did as Fargo had told them, but they didn't look too happy about it.

"Now, then, Butler," Fargo said, "you pick up my gun with the fingers of your left hand and bring it over here. If you try to get fancy, I'll have to punch a sizeable hole in your friend Sullivan's neck."

Butler, who was the bigger of the two men, bent over awkwardly and took hold of the pistol. Holding it gingerly in his fingertips, he carried it to the cell. Fargo reached out and took it with one hand, keeping up a steady pressure on the knife with the other.

When he had the pistol in hand, he said, "I appreciate your help, Butler, I'm sure Deputy Marshal Sullivan does, too. Now it's your turn, Barlow. Come over here and open the door."

Barlow was holding a ring of heavy keys in his hand, but instead of opening the door, he looked at Sullivan.

Fargo gave a little shove with the knife and jabbed the Colt into Sullivan's back for encouragement.

"Open the goddamn door," Sullivan said. He no longer sounded angry, just resigned to the situation.

Barlow fumbled around, jingling the keys, until he found the right one. He put it in the lock and turned it. Sullivan, with a little more encouragement from Fargo, pushed the door open.

When they were both outside the cell, Fargo gestured with his pistol and said, "Now it's your turn. Get on in there. All of you."

There was a spark of anger in Sullivan's eye, and for just a second Fargo thought the three of them might rush him. But the moment passed, the spark died, and Sullivan led the others into the cell. Fargo closed the door behind them and locked it.

"I'll leave the keys outside on the deck," he said. "If you want to come after me again, you can, but remember this: I didn't kill Jim Taylor, and I don't have any idea who did.

There are plenty of people who'll swear that I was never anywhere near him. So find yourselves somebody else to lock
up."

Fargo left them there and went out, dropping the keys on
the desk as he'd promised.

He hadn't been telling the whole truth, he thought, as he
walked through the door and out into the crowded street. He
did have an idea about who'd killed Jim Taylor. After all, who
was the only person in town who might want to frame him for
murder?

He thought it was about time that he paid a little visit to the
Gypsy Queen and met the woman who called herself Esmeralda.

5

He was sidetracked on his way to the saloon when he noticed a small crowd gathered at a street corner. Standing out above the crowd was Alfred Nelson, not because he was tall, which he wasn't, but because he must have been standing on a box. He was still wearing his black suit, and was waving a Bible above his head. He was shouting to make himself heard above the noise of the street, but Fargo couldn't quite make out the words because of all the hubbub. There were miners laughing and talking and teamsters yelling. A pack of dogs barked as they chased a gray cat down an alley. Wheels creaked and wagons groaned under their loads.

Fargo made his way down to the corner to see if he could catch a little of Nelson's message. The little man had worked himself into quite a lather, and he was just concluding his sermon—or whatever it was—when Fargo got there.

"And that's the way it is," Fargo heard him say. "There's heaven high, waiting for you if you follow the narrow path, but woe unto him who follows the broad and easy path that leads straight to the grave and from there right down to hell! Jesus Christ hung on the cross to save every one of you, and you'll never have another day's worry in your life if you take up your cross and follow him down the sure road that leads to salvation. Amen!"

There were a few halfhearted *amens* from the group of men who'd gathered to listen, but there wasn't any enthusiasm in any of them. Fargo thought they'd come more for the entertainment than for the salvation that Nelson was preaching.

When the crowd started to move away, Nelson called out, "Brother Fargo! It's good to see you here."

The preacher jumped down off his box and walked over to

Fargo, sticking out his right hand while he clutched his Bible in the left.

Fargo shook hands and said, "You didn't have much of a congregation."

Nelson waved a hand as if to brush away a pesky fly.

"I'm just getting started," he said. "Besides, the Lord's not interested in numbers. If I can touch one single solitary soul, I've done my duty. If I just opened one ear to the word of the Gospel, I've done as much as any man could."

Fargo interrupted him before he got rolling.

"You have a church yet?"

Nelson grinned and pointed to the wooden box he'd been standing on.

"That's it right there. I know it's not much, but I'll have a better one soon. I've got a line on a tent that I can use starting on Sunday, and before you know it I'll have a brand-new building to preach in. You'll see."

Fargo said he was sure that was true. Then he added, "What do you hear from the rest of the men who came out with us? Ever see any of them?"

"They're too busy staking out claims, hoping to lay up treasures on earth," Nelson said. "They should know that moth and dust will corrupt the treasures of the world. The only sure thing is the love of the Lord."

"So they don't come to hear you preach."

"No more than you do. Except for Jim Taylor. He came around once or twice. But then he's not mining like the others."

That was news to Fargo. He said, "Why not?"

Nelson walked over to his box, motioning for Fargo to follow him. The little preacher took hold of the edge of the box and dragged it up against the wall of the dry goods store in front of which he'd been preaching.

"If I don't watch out," he said, "somebody will carry it off."

Fargo nodded. People weren't particular about what they stole. They'd even take a preacher's empty box, and all Nelson's sermons wouldn't change that.

"Now, what about Taylor," Fargo said when they were well out of the way of the traffic.

"You probably remember that he didn't come out here to get rich," Nelson said. "He just wanted to get away from a bad situation."

He didn't make it, though, Fargo thought.

"I remember," he said. "He didn't like the idea of the war."

"That's right. He didn't really care about money. So he just took a job, working at one of the mines. In the stamp mill."

"Which one?"

"The Silver Emperor, I believe. I might not have the name exactly right. He just mentioned it in passing."

Something in the way he said it made Fargo wonder if he was telling the truth. But would a preacher lie? And if he would, why?

"Why all this interest in Taylor?" Nelson asked. "I didn't know you'd developed a friendship with anybody on the trip out here."

"We weren't friends," Fargo said. "In fact, I was just arrested for his murder."

Nelson's face paled. "Murder? But why would you kill him?"

"I didn't," Fargo said. "But somebody did, and tried to put the blame on me."

"But who would do a terrible thing like that?"

"That's what I'm going to find out," Fargo told him.

It didn't take Fargo long to find out that there was no mine named the Silver Emperor in Virginia City. But there was one called the Silver King. That was probably the one. Fargo was going to pay a visit there, but first he wanted to have a look at the Gypsy Queen. He couldn't persuade Nelson to come along with him. One visit to a saloon was all the preacher needed to last him a long time.

Fargo thought he'd better do one other thing before looking up Esmeralda, however. He'd better let Marian know that he wasn't locked up any longer.

When he got to the Iron Dog, it was getting late in the afternoon, and Marian wasn't anywhere to be seen. Ray, the bartender, told Fargo that she'd gone to talk to a lawyer, if she could find one who was sober.

"She'll be surprised you got out without her help," Ray said. "What happened, anyway?"

"You don't want to hear about it," Fargo said. "When Marian comes back, tell her that things are fine and that I'm not a wanted man anymore."

He wasn't sure that was true, but he didn't think Sullivan would want to try arresting him again, at least not until some time had passed.

"Why can't you tell her?" Ray asked.

"Because I'll be over at the Gypsy Queen," Fargo told him.

"Marian won't like that."

Fargo listened to Glenn play a few bars of some song he didn't recognize. Fargo didn't know whether he didn't recognize it because he just didn't know it or because the piano was so out of tune that nobody could have figured out what song Glenn was playing.

"It doesn't really matter what Marian likes," Fargo said. "I'll be at the Gypsy Queen."

Ray shrugged. "Suit yourself."

"I will," Fargo said.

Fargo walked through the crowd on the boardwalk with a long, loping stride. He didn't like anyone having the idea that Marian controlled him. He was his own man, even when he was working for someone else. Maybe it was time he left Virginia City and got back out into open country. He didn't like towns, anyway. They closed in on him like a trap.

But he didn't want to leave yet, not while there was someone who was trying to set him up to look like a killer. He wasn't going to be chased out of town. He needed to find out what was going on and put a stop to it.

The Gypsy Queen was not an imposing building, no more than the Iron Dog was, and there weren't nearly as many customers around, Fargo saw when he pushed through the batwings and entered.

Marian had been right about the girls, too. They were older and a bit unkempt compared to the women working at the Iron Dog. They were also more aggressive. One of them came up to Fargo before he'd taken three steps inside.

"Hello, big fella," she said. "Looking for a little fun?"

"I'm looking for Esmeralda," Fargo said. "How much fun is she?"

"Not near as much fun as I am," the woman said. "Want to find out?"

She was thin almost to the point of emaciation, all knobs and bones, and her teeth were bad. Fargo wondered how long it had been since she'd had a bath.

"I'd take you up on that," Fargo said, "but I'm here on business."

"Business? Well, I guess that's different. What's your name, anyway?"

"Skye Fargo. Why don't you tell Esmeralda I'm here."

Something in the woman's bleary eyes changed when she heard Fargo's name, and she was suddenly eager to be away from him.

"I'll do that," she said. "Why don't you sit down and have a drink. On the house."

Fargo didn't want a drink, but he didn't get a chance to say so. The woman had already turned away and was hurrying toward a door at the back of the big room.

Fargo went over to a table and sat down. While he waited, he looked around the room. The miners here looked morose and tired compared to the ones who came to the Iron Dog. There were some men gambling at a table in the back, but they didn't appear to have their hearts in it. There was a saloon girl by every chair, trying to cheer them up and not doing much good. Fargo wondered why the atmosphere was so depressing, and decided that maybe it was because Esmeralda didn't have a piano, or music of any kind. Even an out-of-tune piano could brighten things up a little bit. It might not be very musical, but it gave the illusion of music and made people happy for at least a little while.

While Fargo was thinking about that, a woman came out of the back room. She wasn't beautiful, but she didn't miss it by much. She was tall and willowy, with a mass of midnight-black hair that tumbled to her shoulders. She had black eyes, too, and dark olive skin. If she wasn't a gypsy, she certainly looked like one. Her generous mouth was smiling broadly as she approached Fargo's table.

"So zee great Fargo has decided to pay a visit to my 'umble saloon," she said. "I am honored."

Fargo stood up and said, "You must be Esmeralda."

"But of course," she said. "What can I do for you?"

"There seems to be a problem between you and the woman I'm working for. I thought it might be a good idea for us to talk about it."

"And why should *we* talk?"

"Because you sent a man to shoot up the Iron Dog not long ago and because today I was arrested for murder. Those are two pretty good reasons, I think."

"I do not know what you are talking about," Esmeralda said. "You are mistaken if you think I had anything to do with those incidents. I keep a saloon. I do not send men to 'shoot up,' as you say, the other place of business."

Esmeralda was quite an actress. Fargo thought that with her good looks, she could make more money on the stage than she was making in the saloon business.

"Then why did Slade say you'd sent him?" he asked.

"Slade? I do not know zeez Slade."

"I'll tell you what," Fargo said. "Let's you and I go somewhere private. I don't want to say anymore out here in front of these people."

"There are not many here," Esmeralda said. "It is a great disappointment to me."

"I'm sure it is. No wonder you sent Slade over to the Iron Dog with his shotgun."

Esmeralda looked for a second as if she were going to deny it again, but she didn't. She said, "Come along, then, if that is what you wish. We can talk in my office."

She turned, and without looking to see if he was following, she walked back toward the door from which she'd entered the room. Fargo stood for a moment to admire the way her hips moved under her dress. She had a sensuous body, and he wouldn't mind seeing more of it if the opportunity presented itself. After a second, he went after her.

As soon as Fargo entered the office, Esmeralda said, "Shut zee door."

Fargo did as he was told and then looked around the room. There was a small, worn desk, a couple of chairs, and a sofa.

There was no rug on the floor. He turned to Esmeralda and said, "Where were you born? It was somewhere east of the Mississippi."

"Yes. It was far east of there. It was in a small country across the sea, where the gypsies roam free and take what they want from others."

"You might find some people around here who'll believe that," Fargo said. "But I'm not one of them."

"How dare you insult me!"

She came at him, her hand raised as if to slap him. Fargo caught her wrist and twisted her arm behind her back, pulling her close to him. He could feel the softness of her breasts and see the fire in her eyes.

"Let me go!" she said, but she wasn't struggling at all. In fact, she was pushing herself even closer to Fargo, letting him feel the warm length of her. The look in her eyes was a challenge of a kind that Fargo was familiar with.

He knew, however, that he was in a precarious position and that Esmeralda was a dangerous woman. She knew exactly what she was doing. If she couldn't stop Marian one way, she'd try another.

What Fargo couldn't quite make up his mind about was whether to let her make the try. He was still considering it when Esmeralda put her free hand behind his head and brought his mouth down to hers.

Her kiss was as fiery as her eyes, and Fargo found himself joining in the game with enthusiasm. Esmeralda rubbed her body against him and made a sound that was almost like a cat purring.

What the hell, Fargo thought. Marian paid him a salary, but she didn't own him. Besides, he might find Esmeralda in a talkative mood after a little session on the sofa that just happened to be so near at hand. Fargo wondered how many men Esmeralda had led to that sofa, but he decided that it didn't matter.

Esmeralda stepped back and smiled.

"Do you like me better now?" she asked.

"I never said I didn't like you," Fargo told her.

"That is true. But you were accusing me falsely."

Esmeralda undid something at the back of her dress and

41

suddenly she stood there wearing nothing but her underthings. Fargo looked at her admiringly.

"You like what you see, yes?"

"I like what I see," Fargo said. "Yes."

"But you would like to see more?"

"That sounds fine," Fargo said. "Do you want to show me?"

"Oh, yes. I do."

She moved quickly, and before Fargo could think of anything to say, she was standing before him completely naked. She cupped her breasts in her hands as if offering them to him. They were fine and firm, and if they were smaller than Marian's, they were no less attractive, tipped with large nipples that were very brown and very hard. The thatch of curls at the junction of her thighs was thick and black.

"Does your Marian have anything like these?" Esmeralda asked.

Fargo was tempted to say that while Esmeralda's breasts were very nice, every woman had something like them. But he didn't think that was what Esmeralda wanted to hear. So he said nothing and started taking his own clothes off.

As he undressed, Esmeralda walked across the room and locked the door. When she walked her hips swayed sensuously, the cheeks of her buttocks clenching and unclenching with each step.

When she turned back, Fargo had his clothes off, and Esmeralda gave him a slow up and down. Then she let out a slow, soft whistle.

"I knew you were tall," she said. "But sometimes tall does not mean big. I am glad that in your case, it does."

She walked to him and took his hand, leading him to the couch. He was about to pull her down on it, but she didn't give him a chance. She let go of his hands and gave him a gentle push.

"Sit down and rest a while," she said.

Fargo did as he was told, sitting on the couch with his stiff pole sticking up between his legs. Esmeralda dropped to her knees in front of him and took hold of his shaft, running her hand slowly up and down the entire length of it.

42

"It is very red," she said. "As if it were on fire. But I know how to quench it."

She leaned forward and took him in her mouth, enveloping him in the heat of it. His fingers tangled in her hair as she moved her head in a way that sent sweet sensations right to Fargo's backbone. He found himself almost rising off the couch each time she raised her head.

After a while, she looked up and smiled.

"Now," she said, "it is your turn."

She sat on the couch and spread her legs. Fargo dropped to the floor and began to tease her with his tongue. She braced herself on the sofa with her arms rigid on each side of her body and arched her back with pleasure. Her long black hair hung down behind her, and Fargo continued to let his tongue explore. Fargo darted his tongue at the ridge of flesh again and again. Each time it made contact, Esmeralda twitched, and each time she moaned deep in her throat.

After a few more seconds, it appeared that she could stand it no longer. She raised Fargo's head and said, "I want you now, Fargo. Hurry!"

She turned on the sofa and Fargo lifted himself on top of her. She reached for him as if to guide him inside her, but instead she tickled the tip of his shaft with the wiry hair at her entrance, and after a moment of that rubbed it hard against her opening. When she could take no more she led him through the gates and held her breath as he found his way home.

"Ohhhh," she said. *"Yessssss."*

They both began to move, slowly at first and then faster and faster as they both neared the peak of their pleasure. Esmeralda, flushed with heat, started to shudder. As Fargo was about to withdraw, she locked her ankles behind him and pulled him tightly to her. She held him there while spasm after spasm of pleasure shook her.

"Ah-ah-ah-ah-ah!" she said.

When she loosened her grip, Fargo pulled out to the tip, then drove back into her fast and hard. His own climax cannoned into her, shot after shot, each round sending new waves of ecstasy rippling through her screams and moans. "Yes! Yes! Yes!"

When it was over, they were both exhausted. Fargo rolled

away and sat up. Esmeralda did the same, leaning back with her hair fanned out on the back of the sofa.

"You're better than I expected, Fargo. Much better. I don't blame Marian for hiring you. Is there anything I could do to get you to work here instead?"

"I'm not a stud service," Fargo said. "I take my pleasure where I please."

"God knows that's the truth. I had no intention of doing what we just did, but one thing just seemed to lead to another, and there we were."

Fargo didn't believe that for a minute, though he did notice that there was one thing that might indicate something resembling sincerity: Her accent was gone.

"Where are you from, really," Fargo said.

She considered him for a second or two and said, "Missouri. What about you?"

"Nowhere," Fargo said. "And everywhere. I move around a lot. Always have."

She let her fingers play over his body.

"What about the scars?"

"That one's from a bear," Fargo said. "He almost got the best of me."

"But he didn't, did he?"

"Nope. He looks worse than I do. Or he would if he were still alive. He's not."

"You're not afraid of very much, I'd guess."

"Then you'd guess wrong. A man who says he's never been afraid is either a fool or a liar. I'd like to think that I'm neither."

"Well if you're afraid, you don't let it stop you, do you?"

"It depends on what I'm after," Fargo said.

"That's what I thought. And I guess you came here after something that you don't have yet."

"That's right," Fargo said. "But I enjoyed what I did get."

Esmeralda laughed. "So did I. You do know how to make a lady feel good."

While she was feeling so friendly, Fargo said, "Now tell me about Slade."

Esmeralda stopped laughing and her mouth tightened.

"I thought we went over that a while ago."

44

"We did. But that was before we became such good friends."

Esmeralda laughed again, her good mood returning.

"I like you, Fargo. I really do. I wish I had a man like you working for me instead of a man like Slade."

"So he does work for you."

"Yes. I sent him to the Iron Dog. Why should Marian have all the business? My place is as nice as hers. Maybe nicer. Why don't I have more customers?"

Fargo decided that he might as well tell her. She probably knew anyway.

"Because you let the gamblers cheat, your girls aren't very attractive, and you don't even have a piano. And you water the drinks."

"I do not water the drinks!"

"Maybe you don't, but somebody does. At least that's what people say. And the other things are all true, too."

"So if I changed all that, my business would improve?"

"It's better than sending a tinhorn gambler or a man with a shotgun. Why don't you try it and see?"

"Maybe I will," Esmeralda said. She paused. "Marian would hate you if she knew what we had done."

"I'm not planning to tell her," Fargo said. "And you're not either."

"I guess not. I hope we'll get a chance to do it again."

"So do I," Fargo said. "But I might be in jail."

"Jail? Why would you be in jail?"

"Because someone told Deputy Marshal Sullivan that I killed a man named Jim Taylor."

Fargo watched Esmeralda closely as he told her about Taylor. Either she was a better actress than he'd thought, or she knew nothing about the murder."

"Did you?" Esmeralda asked. "Kill him, I mean."

"No," Fargo said. "I didn't. But I'm going to find out who did."

The way he said it seemed to put a chill in Esmeralda.

"I believe you will," she said.

6

The big news in Virginia City the next day was the stage robbery. Not that it was anything unusual. In fact, the stage was robbed so frequently that it would have been bigger news if it hadn't been robbed, or so Fargo was told by Glenn during a break from his piano playing.

"They took the silver again," Glenn said.

It was morning, and things were slow in the Iron Dog. Glenn and Fargo sat at one of the vacant tables, and Fargo toyed idly with a poker chip that someone had left there.

"Silver leaves here all the time, of course," Glenn said. "It's not like everybody doesn't know it. What they need is more protection."

"Were the passengers robbed?" Fargo asked, walking the poker chip across the backs of the fingers on his right hand.

"They're always robbed," Glenn said. "But I don't think the robbers are after what the passengers are carrying. It doesn't amount to much compared to the silver."

"Where can they go with the silver?" Fargo asked.

"What?"

"It's heavy. They'd need something to carry it in, a wagon maybe. And then they'd have to sell it. Where could they go?"

"I see what you mean," Glenn said. "California, I guess. They could get rid of it there."

"Maybe," Fargo said. "Seems like a lot of hard work."

"It would be worth it," Glenn said. "Those bars are worth plenty, and taking them to California wouldn't be hard at all, not with some men and a wagon."

"You're probably right," Fargo said. "And speaking of silver, I'm going to pay a visit to a mine."

"What for? You looking for another job?"

Fargo didn't see that it was any of Glenn's business one way or the other. So he said, "Because I haven't seen one since I've been here. A man ought not to spend so much time in Virginia City without having a look at a silver mine."

"I see what you mean," Glenn said, but it was clear that he didn't.

Fargo didn't have far to go; he thought he'd just walk. No need to get his horse out of the stable for such a short trip. The truth was, nowhere in Virginia City was far from anywhere else, and most of the mines were practically right in town. Many of their tunnels ran right underneath it.

As it turned out, the trip wasn't long, but it was uphill. Fargo still wasn't used to the lack of oxygen at this altitude, and he found himself getting a little short of breath as he trudged along. He was glad he didn't have far to go.

While he was walking, he thought about Marian and her reaction to his little visit to the Gypsy Queen. She hadn't been as upset as he'd thought. In fact, she really hadn't seemed to mind at all, especially when he explained that he'd persuaded Esmeralda not to send Slade back.

"Now that's good news," Marian had said. "I hope she keeps her promise."

Fargo explained that Esmeralda hadn't exactly promised. And that she was planning to try to build up her business by honest means.

"Let her try. I've still got the best place in town. She won't take any of my customers."

Fargo wasn't so sure, but he didn't want to argue about it.

"What about Sullivan?" Marian asked. "By the time I got old Lawyer Johnson sobered up and got him to the jail, you were already gone. And Sullivan was in a very dark mood. I think he'd have shot me if he'd thought he could get away with it."

Fargo told her what had happened, and Marian had a good laugh.

"It's nothing more than Sullivan deserves," she said. "From what I hear, he's no better than an outlaw himself. He's committed more than one murder in this town, but he's never been arrested or jailed. After all, he's supposed to be the law. You'd better watch your back, Fargo. That man is out to get you, one way or another."

Fargo had assured her that he'd watch his back, and no more was said about either Esmeralda or Sullivan, for which Fargo was just as glad.

There was nothing imposing about the Silver King, and nothing to set it apart from any of the other mines in the area, some of which were producing a lot, some of which were producing little. From what Fargo had heard, the Silver King was one of those producing a lot.

There was a mine shaft that opened into the mountain, a gaping black hole shored up by timbers. Nearby stood a few scattered cabins where some of the miners could bunk, in addition to one that served as an office. All of them were made of raw, unpainted planks. A couple of carts were outside the entrance, and Fargo saw the tracks that went down into the mine. There was a cookshed, too, and a Chinese cook was standing outside it. When he saw Fargo, he turned and went in. An eight-stamp mill was located nearby, and it was pounding away.

Fargo stood and looked things over for a minute or so before heading for the office. Before he got there, however, a short, stocky man came through the door and headed for the cookshed.

"Wong!" he yelled. "Wong, you bastard, you come out of there."

Fargo decided that any man who talked like that to the hired help must be the boss. He fell in a few steps behind him and followed him to the shed, though he moved so quietly that the man didn't hear him.

Before they got there, Wong came outside. He was dressed in a white smock and wore a white puffy hat atop his head.

"Whassa mattah?" he asked as he emerged. "Boss not happy with Wong? What Wong do?"

"You cooked the goddamn' biscuits too hard again," the stocky man said. "The boys are complaining. Said they were likely to break a tooth on the damn' things. If you don't do better, I'll fire your ass."

"Wong always try to do best he can. Wong just poor Chinaman."

"Wong a son of a bitch," the man said, drawing back his arm to belt the cook in the face.

Fargo took a couple of steps and took hold of the arm. The man turned around, surprise and anger in his face.

"Who the hell are you?" he said. He jerked his arm free. "And what the hell are you doing on my property?"

"Name's Fargo," Fargo said. "And I came looking for a friend of mine who works for you."

"I'm Sam King," the man said, eyeing Fargo suspiciously. He didn't offer his hand. "This here is my mine, and I don't like strangers prowling around."

Wong grinned at Fargo over King's shoulder, as if pleased to have King's attention turned elsewhere, and took the opportunity to move quietly back into the cookshed.

"I'm pleased to meet you, Mr. King," Fargo said. "I'm not prowling around. Like I said, I'm looking for a friend."

"I know what you said. Who's this friend of yours?"

"Jim Taylor," Fargo said.

King spat on the ground. "He worked for me about three days. Left without drawing his wages, and I ain't seen him since. Don't know where he went, and I don't give a damn. Now get off my property before I have you run off."

"Somebody killed him," Fargo said.

"Then he probably needed killing. Ain't none of my business what happened to him. A man that walks off his job without giving notice is pretty sorry if you ask me. Are you gonna leave, or do I have to make you."

"I'll go," Fargo said, wondering why King was so hostile. Maybe it was the hard biscuits. He also wondered about Taylor. From what Fargo had learned about him on their journey, it didn't seem like Taylor was the type to have walked off the job. He was a man with firm convictions about right and wrong, the kind of man who liked to see his obligations through. He wouldn't just walk away without giving any reason.

Fargo hadn't gotten far before he heard Wong yelling. Turning back, Fargo saw that King was dragging Wong out of the cookshed, holding onto a black pigtail that grew halfway down Wong's back. When they were outside, King released

49

the pigtail, and Wong fell on the ground, where King started kicking him and cursing with each kick.

"Goddamn' heathen son of a bitch," King yelled.

Fargo was tempted to go right on back to town. He'd already interfered in one fight in Virginia City, and while he'd gotten a job as a result, he'd also been tossed in the hoosegow. Maybe it would be better if he just walked away.

He thought about it, but he couldn't do it. Wong's trouble wasn't his trouble, but it just didn't seem right to let a big man beat up on a little man like that. Fargo went back.

His years on the trail had given Fargo the ability to move quietly and unobtrusively. King didn't see or hear him this time, either, not until it was too late to do anything about it. Still, he paused in midkick to go for the pistol he had strapped to his side.

Fargo didn't give him a chance to get it. He took hold of King's wrist and held it where it was, with the gun about halfway drawn.

"You ought not to kick a man when he's down," Fargo said.

"He's my man," King said, straining to move his hand. "And I'll do with him as I damn well please."

"I don't think it would be a good idea," Fargo said.

King didn't answer. He braced his feet and shoved Fargo as hard as he could.

Fargo fell backward, but he didn't release his hold on King's wrist. He landed on his back and threw King over and past him. By the time King landed, Fargo was on his feet again.

King twisted around, clawing for his pistol, but when he looked up, he was staring into the barrel of Fargo's Colt.

"You can go ahead and draw if you want to," Fargo told him, "but I don't really think it would be a good idea."

King apparently didn't think so either. He moved his hand away from the gun and sat there looking at Fargo.

"You sure do like messing in people's business," King said. "It's going to cause you some trouble one of these days."

"I expect so," Fargo said, not bothering to mention the troubles it had already caused him.

"I could have you shot right now," King said, "and not a soul would know the difference."

Fargo said, "You must be forgetting who's holding the gun. And Wong would know the difference."

King laughed. "Who'd believe a Chinaman? And you ain't the only one holding a gun, or hadn't you noticed?"

He turned his head and looked over at the office building. Fargo saw that one window was open and that someone was standing in the shadows inside. He couldn't tell who it was, couldn't even tell if it was a man or a woman. The shotgun poking out the window wasn't in the shadows, however. Fargo could see it just fine.

"Little far away for a shotgun," Fargo said. "Be as likely to hit you as to hit me."

"Maybe," King said, "but I don't see any need for us to find that out, do you?"

Fargo said he didn't think so and holstered his pistol. He looked around for Wong, but once again he'd managed to disappear.

"Don't come back here," King said, getting to his feet. "If you show up again, you won't get any warning. You'll just get shot."

There was something in the way he said it that eliminated any cause for doubt. Fargo wondered again why the man seemed so upset. Just because he'd been interrupted while beating his cook? Because the biscuits were too hard? Or was there more to it?

Fargo decided that it didn't really matter. Whatever it was, he'd leave it be. Jim Taylor was a good enough man, but he wasn't any real friend of Fargo's. And Fargo didn't think Sullivan would be arresting him again for the killing. There had probably been one or two more murders in Virginia City by this time.

Fargo shook his head and went on back to town, back to the Iron Dog.

Two days later, somebody killed the preacher.

Nelson had built up a little reputation for himself, so the news of his murder created more of a stir than Taylor's had. People talked about it on the street, and there was a big story about it in the *Territorial Enterprise*.

"You see this?" Glenn asked Fargo that afternoon, showing him the newspaper. "Didn't you know that preacher fella?"

Fargo didn't make it a habit to read newspapers. He could read, but he just didn't see the point. Seemed like the news was always pretty much the same. A silver strike here, a dead man there. The names changed, but the details didn't differ much.

This story was different, though, since it was about some-one Fargo knew. He read it, but he didn't find out much. Nelson had been shot down at night, in an alley not far from the Chinese section. Deputy Marshal Sullivan was on the job, and he naturally suspected that one of the Chinese had killed Nelson, probably because he'd offended their heathen gods. Or so the story said. Fargo wondered how long it would be before Sullivan made the connection between Fargo and Nelson, or if he'd even bother to investigate. After all, he could arrest any Chinaman in town and nobody would care. Nobody except other Chinamen, and they were less than nothing as far as the law and the other citizens of Virginia City were concerned.

Fargo handed the paper back to Glenn.

"I knew him," Fargo said. "He was with a party I brought out here from Missouri. Funny he'd get killed like that. He was handy enough with a gun."

"You think Sullivan will be in to arrest you again?"

"I don't think so," Fargo said. "I think he already has some-body in mind."

"Yeah," Glenn said, losing interest in the topic. "Can't blame him for that. You just can't trust those Chinamen."

Fargo nodded. "That's what they say."

Other people were a lot more concerned about Nelson's death than Glenn seemed to be, perhaps because they felt more intimately involved. That night, Fargo had some visitors at the saloon: Carl Edwards, Waymon Carter, and Lane Utley.

Of the three, Edwards was doing the best. He hadn't found any silver, but it hadn't taken him long to discover that he didn't need to.

"I'm making more money cutting hair than I could dig out of the ground," he told Fargo. "The miners that have money like to get spiffed up every now and then, and they're willing

52

to pay for a good cut and a shave. I got on with another barber, and we're doing just fine."

Carter and Utley were still sticking to their goal of finding silver, and they were working together.

"We've got us a couple of claims," Utley said. "You never know what you might turn up. Look at the Ophir. They're taking enough silver out of there every day to fill up this saloon. If we hit it big, we'll be doing the same."

Fargo thought that the odds of that happening were about the same as him finding gold nuggets under his bed every night. He said, "I guess it could happen like that."

"Sure it could," Carter said. "Look at that Sam King. He got started out with not much more than Lane and me, and now he's a rich man. Won't be long before he'll be building a mansion in San Francisco."

They talked about that for a while, and about some of the other big strikes, but Fargo knew that wasn't why they'd come there. They were drinking beer, but they hadn't come for that either. And they sure hadn't come for the piano music. Fargo didn't want to rush them, though. The more beer they drank, the better it was for Marian's business.

It took two beers each and part of a third, but finally they got around to the reason for their visit. It was Utley who brought it up, and Fargo reckoned he'd been appointed the spokesman before they ever got to the Iron Dog.

"I guess you heard about somebody killing Nelson," Utley said.

Fargo told them that he'd heard. "Read about it in the newspaper," he said.

The men looked at one another. They obviously hadn't thought about the newspaper. They'd just heard people talking.

"Why would anybody want to do a thing like that?" Utley asked. "Nelson was a preacher. He never hurt anybody."

"Newspaper says it was the Chinese," Fargo told them. "Maybe Nelson was preaching against their religion."

"That's what somebody said. You ever hear him preach?"

"Once," Fargo said. "A few days ago."

"Then you know he wasn't preaching against anybody's religion," Edwards said. "He was just preaching like any other preacher, trying to get a few sinners to see the light. He didn't say anything about any Chinamen. They're just trying to find somebody to blame, and the Chinamen are handy. You don't really think a Chinaman killed Taylor do you?"

"Maybe not," Fargo said. "But what's all this got to do with me?"

"It's not just you," Utley said. "It's me and Edwards and Carter, too."

"What makes you think so?"

"You know about Taylor," Utley said. "I know you do because you got arrested when he was killed."

Fargo nodded, not sure where this was headed. But he was beginning to get an idea.

"Well, somebody killed him and now somebody's killed Nelson," Utley said. "Don't that strike you as funny?"

"This is a mining town," Fargo said. "It's on the boom. People get murdered here all the time. It can even happen to a preacher."

"Nelson was backshot," Carter put in. "You ever hear of a Chinaman backshootin' a man? They like a knife, from what I hear."

"What he means is that it seems a little funny for two men from the same party to get killed so close together like that," Utley said. "It's like somebody's got it in for us."

Fargo thought it over. There might have been three of the party dead if he'd stayed in that cell with Sullivan much longer. You could dismiss two from the same group as a coincidence, but three would harder to explain. He wasn't dead, though, and he wasn't sure Sullivan wanted to kill him. Sullivan just wanted to make him hurt a lot.

"I don't see what we can do about it," he said. "Except be sure we watch our backs."

"That ain't good enough for us," Utley said. He looked around at Carter and Edwards, who nodded in agreement. "We think we oughta do something about it."

"Like what?" Fargo asked.

"Well, that's where you come in," Utley said. "I'm just a farmer, and Edwards cuts hair. Carter there, well, he was a justice of the peace back home, but he don't know a thing about murders. Probably wasn't ever a murder in that little town where he comes from. That right, Carter?"

Carter said that it was. "Had a suicide once. But the man was a bad drunk. Nobody was surprised. No question about him killing himself. This here, this is a lot different from that."

"I still don't see what you want me to do about it," Fargo said.

"We want you to find out who killed them," Utley said. "That's what. And we want you to put a stop to it before it happens to one of us."

"Oh," Fargo said.

7

Fargo thought about it after the men left. They hadn't been able to come up with a reason why anyone would want to kill them. They hadn't known each other particularly well in Missouri, and they didn't have any enemies in common, certainly nobody who would have followed them to Nevada Territory to kill them.

"What about since you got here?" Fargo had asked. "You done anything to make anybody real mad?"

"Me and Utley staked our claims fair and square," Carter said. "There can't be any trouble about that. Besides, we hadn't even seen Taylor since we left this place the first time. We've been by and let Cal shave us a time or two, and that's it. The whole bunch of us went our separate ways, except for me and Utley."

" 'Course we heard Nelson preaching a time or two," Utley said. "It was hard not to if you came to town. He was out there all the time, waving that Bible around."

Fargo asked Edwards about Taylor.

"Hadn't seen him but once since we got here," the big man said. "He came by and got himself a haircut. He didn't say much, though. Didn't seem to want to talk about his job. I saw Nelson on the street now and then, but that was it. We haven't got together or anything like that. I tell you Fargo, I can't figure it."

Of the three, Carter was the most nervous and scared. He kept looking around the whole time they'd talked, as if he expected someone to walk through the batwing doors with a gun in his hand and kill all of them.

"You got to do something, Fargo," he said. "I don't want to

get shot down just when I'm on the verge of making a big strike."

"Me neither," Utley said. "We ain't got much money, Fargo, but we can pay you a little. Besides, you'd be helping yourself out at the same time."

They'd finished their third and fourth beers by the time the discussion was over, and Fargo had agreed to do what he could. He just hadn't been able to figure out what that might be.

"You can do more than the police in this town," Utley said. "I don't trust them for a second."

Fargo couldn't blame Utley for that. He didn't trust them either, Sullivan especially.

Before the men left, Carter pulled Fargo aside and handed him a folded piece of paper.

"What's this?" Fargo asked.

"I got a wife back in St. Jo," Carter said. "And a little girl, too. I came out here because I knew if I stayed there I was never going to amount to anything much, just a local politician without any future. I thought that here I could make a new start and put something together for the future. Thought I could get a nice stake and bring them out West to live with me."

He sounded like a man who never believed that what he was talking about would come to pass.

"You can still do that," Fargo said, trying to encourage him.

"Maybe. Or maybe I'll just get backshot when I walk out of here tonight. That's why I gave you that paper. It's my last will and testament and a letter I wrote to my wife and little girl. I was hoping you might see that they get it if I don't make it."

Fargo couldn't see why Carter was so depressed. There wasn't even any proof that the two killings were connected. But Carter didn't want to hear about proof. He wanted Fargo to make him a promise.

"All right," Fargo said. "I'll see to it that they get it."

"I appreciate it," Carter said, shaking Fargo's free hand. "I'm leaving them my claim, so if I don't get through this, they'll at least have something to count on."

Fargo thought that Carter must have been pretty sure his claim was a good one, though it hadn't shown anything so far.

"That's just because we haven't got deep enough," Carter said when Fargo mentioned it. "This ain't like California, where they used to just scrape the gold up off the ground or pan it out of a creek. You got to go down deep, and me and Utley are just getting started. We'll hit it big, if we don't get killed."

"Good luck, then," Fargo said.

"Thanks," Carter said. "We'll be needing it."

Fargo had another beer. Marian came over and sat down across from him.

"Who're your friends, Fargo?" she asked.

"They're the men I brought out here. Or what's left of them. Somebody's killed two of them, and they can't figure out why. One of them's that preacher, Nelson, who's been out on the streets lately."

"I heard about him. He was all right, for a preacher, at least so far. He hadn't gotten started on the evils of drink and women and gambling yet."

Fargo wondered when Nelson would have gotten around to that. Those seemed like the sorts of things preachers liked to condemn. But then Nelson had been a different kind of a preacher.

"People say a Chinaman killed him," Marian said.

Fargo nodded. "That's what they say. Doesn't mean it's the truth, though. Those three men you saw over here don't think so. They think it's somebody else, somebody who might be after all of them."

"So they asked you to help."

"How'd you know that?" Fargo asked.

"Because you're the kind of man people turn to when they're in trouble," Marian said. "That's what I did, isn't it?"

"I guess it is," Fargo said.

"It's even what Esmeralda did. I hear she's trying to straighten things out at her place since you had that little talk with her." Marian paused and looked across the table at Fargo. "Talk. That's all you did, isn't it?"

"What else would I do?" Fargo asked.

"You know good and well what. I've seen Esmeralda. She might be dishonest, and she might not know much about how

58

to run a saloon, but she's a good-looking woman. And she's just the kind who'd think she could make you see things her way if she took her clothes off for you."

Fargo didn't say anything, and Marian smiled.

"Of course it's none of my business what you did," she said. "Or didn't do. You work for me, but that doesn't mean I have any claim on you. You're your own man, Fargo, and I wouldn't want it any other way."

Fargo was glad to hear it. He'd figured that word of his little encounter with Esmeralda would get out sooner or later, maybe from Esmeralda herself if she wanted to stir up trouble, and it was good to know that Marian had the right idea about things.

"You do what you want to for your friends," Marian told him. "I don't mind if you spend a little time helping them out."

Fargo told her he'd think about it, and she went off to see that the customers were having a good time. Fargo had another beer and thought about the situation some more. As far as he could tell, Marian no longer really needed him around the saloon. There hadn't been any more trouble since he'd taken care of Slade. Come to think of it, Fargo hadn't seen Slade since that time, even though Esmeralda had said he was working for her. Maybe she'd fired him. Or maybe he'd gone out on his own. He'd seemed to Fargo like the sort of fella who might try to strike back by doing something underhanded, like killing a man's friends. Maybe he didn't know that Fargo and the party of men he'd brought to Virginia City weren't really close. Maybe he'd decided to strike back at Fargo by killing the others.

It seemed like a pretty far-fetched idea at first, but the more Fargo thought about it, the more it seemed possible. He thought it might be a good idea to have a little talk with Slade and find out what he'd been doing with himself lately.

Fargo got up and made his way through the tables to where Marian was talking to some miners who were playing cards and enjoying spending their money. As far as he could tell, business in the saloon hadn't fallen off any, even if Esmeralda was trying to straighten things out at the Gypsy Queen.

When Fargo told Marian what he was going to do, she cautioned him to be careful.

"Slade hasn't forgotten what you did to him," she said. "You can count on that. He may not be killing those other men, but he wouldn't hesitate to kill you if he got the chance. Were those others shot in the back?"

Fargo said that they were.

"That could be Slade's work. He doesn't like to face people, and when he does, he doesn't take chances. You saw that scattergun of his."

Fargo told her that he'd be careful, and he went by the piano to tell Glenn that he was going out.

"Nowhere to go at this time of night except another saloon," Glenn said, continuing to play some bouncy tune that Fargo didn't know. "And you ought not to go there."

"I'm just going to find out about a few things," Fargo said. "That's all."

"I wouldn't mind finding out a few things about Esmeralda, myself."

"I'll let you know if there's anything interesting."

"You do that," Glenn said.

There wasn't really much difference between night and day in Virginia City. The night was darker, naturally enough, but the streets were still crowded. The miners worked in shifts since day and night didn't matter down in the tunnels, and men who worked during the day were always ready for a little fun after nightfall. If anything, the crowds were a little more boisterous when the dark closed in.

But even with the people and the noise, there were still dark paths and alleys veering off the main streets, little byways that led to the Chinese quarters or the red-light district on *D* Street. A man who strayed off the main streets could get into all kinds of trouble if he wanted to, or even if he didn't intend it, which Fargo certainly didn't. Not that it mattered. Sometimes a man didn't have to go looking for trouble; it came looking for him.

It came for Fargo when he heard someone say his name.

"Mister Fargo. Mister Fargo."

It wasn't loud, somewhere between a whisper and a normal tone, and it came from an alley that Fargo had just passed. He looked around. There were several people nearby, but nobody he knew. He went back a couple of steps to the entrance to the alley and looked down it.

It was very dark between the wooden buildings, but Fargo could see the silhouette of a man a few yards away.

"Mister Fargo? Is that you?" the man said.

Fargo's hand went to the Colt, and he slid it from its holster.

"Who wants to know?" he asked.

"It is I, Wong, the cook from the Silver King."

Fargo didn't believe it for a minute. Wong had barely been able to speak English, but whoever was in the alley had used better grammar than probably nine-tenths of the population of Virginia City.

"Come on out here, Wong," Fargo said. "Let's have a look at you."

"It is not good for a Chinaman to be seen on the streets at this hour. Please. Come in here and talk. I knew your friend, Jim Taylor."

Now Fargo was getting curious. There weren't very many people who knew of any connection between Fargo and Taylor. There was Sullivan, for one, which reminded Fargo of something he should have thought of before. Who'd told Sullivan that Fargo had known Taylor?

"If you knew Taylor," Fargo said to whoever it was in the alley, "come out and tell me about him."

"I cannot come out, but I will come to the light. You will see that I am who I say."

The man started toward Fargo, who kept his pistol pointed at the dark figure, half expecting to see Slade or Sullivan. But when the man came closer, Fargo saw that it was Wong after all.

"Please," Wong said. "Come with me so that we can talk."

He turned and went back down the alley. Fargo followed, but he didn't holster the pistol. After they had gone far enough to be hidden from the street, Fargo stopped and said, "Why were you talking the way you did at the mine?"

Wong turned. He said, "Because that is the way Mr. King expects a Chinaman to talk. I need my job there, so I do not wish to disappoint him."

Fargo suppressed a laugh. "You have him fooled, all right. Me too."

"I apologize. You are a good man, and you came to help me when very few would have done the same. I would like to help you if I can."

Maybe he was telling the truth. Fargo slipped the Colt back into its holster.

"You said something about Jim Taylor."

"Yes," Wong said. "I overheard you talking to Mr. King. That is how I learned your name and what you had come to the mine for. I liked Mr. Taylor. He treated me like a man and not just some odd stranger with no feelings."

Taylor would have been like that, Fargo thought. He was a good man. Too bad someone had killed him.

"Somebody didn't like him," he told Wong. "Somebody shot him."

"I know. That is what I wanted to tell you. Mr. King knows that, too."

That wasn't the story that King had given Fargo. He'd said that Taylor walked off the job and hadn't come back. So now Fargo knew that King was a liar. Or Wong was. One or the other.

"Why would King lie to me?" Fargo asked.

"That is what I cannot answer," Wong said. "But there are others who might know."

Fargo was going to ask who these "others" might be when he heard a noise from the dark end of the alley. It wasn't much of a noise, not much more than the brushing of an arm against the side of a building, but Fargo's senses were always alert, and he looked past Wong's shoulder to see what had caused the sound.

There was a movement in the dark, and Fargo said, "Let's get out of here."

He turned for the light and the street just as two men stepped into the mouth of the alley. Both held pistols, and both looked as if they knew what to do with them.

"Come this way," Wong said, grabbing Fargo's shoulder.

Fargo turned and followed Wong again, figuring that the devil he didn't know might be better than the devil he did. The two men both fired at their backs. One bullet cracked the wall to Fargo's left, and the other must have nicked Wong, who cried out and stumbled, but kept going.

Someone stepped into the back of the alley from a doorway and said, "Stop right there."

Fargo didn't stop, and neither did Wong. The man raised a gun to his shoulder, but Fargo had his Colt out by then and got off two shots. The first one drove the man back into the doorway. The second one cut him down.

Fire came from the men behind, but Fargo and Wong had reached the end of the alley. Wong turned left, and Fargo went after him. If Wong was hurt, it hadn't slowed him down any. Fargo found himself hard-pressed to keep up. He told himself that he just wasn't used to the altitude.

He followed Wong down a winding course, and before long they were in the Chinese section of the town. The streets were so narrow that a wagon couldn't pass through them, and the houses were crowded together tightly. There were scents in the air that Fargo didn't recognize, strange cooking odors, and the smell of laundry.

That didn't discourage the men who were chasing him. They had somehow managed to follow along, and they burst into the street with blazing guns. They missed Fargo and Wong, but a man standing to the side fell with a bullet in his head.

The streets miraculously emptied. Fargo could hardly credit his eyesight. Where there had been many men and women only seconds before, there was now no one except the dead man. And of course the gunmen who seemed bent on killing Fargo and Wong for some reason.

"In here," Wong said, pulling Fargo's arm to direct him through a door.

Almost as soon as they were inside the building, Fargo knew they wouldn't be disturbing anybody. Young men and old men sat or reclined with half-open mouths and closed eyes, and the pipes that they held or that had been dropped beside them didn't contain tobacco.

Wong closed the door and locked it.

"Opium," he said. "It is not good, but some men need it."

In the dim light, Fargo could see that a bullet had torn through the top of Wong's shoulder. The wound wasn't bleeding much, and it didn't look to be serious. Fargo didn't have time to think about it because the gunmen were banging on the door.

"This way," Wong said, leading Fargo through the tangle of bodies.

Not a person there seemed in the least bit curious about why two men were running through the house. Not a person seemed to care.

There was a stairway at the back of the room, and Wong led the way up. Fargo had gotten about half way when he heard gunshots. The men were taking care of the lock.

Wong ran along a hallway at the top of the stairs, Fargo right behind. If it had been up to Fargo, he would have stood and fought, but he didn't want to lose Wong, who must know something. If he didn't, why were those men trying to kill him?

On the other hand, maybe they weren't. Maybe they were trying to kill Fargo. It was something he'd have to work out later.

Wong opened a window at the end of the hall and jumped out. He landed on the roof of the building next door, straightened, and looked back up for Fargo, who landed right beside him.

"You seem to know your way around here," Fargo said.

"I know many people and places. But we can talk later."

Wong ran across the roof. Fargo was almost over the edge when a bullet took a chunk out of the wood beside him. He looked back at one of the gunmen, who was standing at the open window. Fargo didn't wait for him to shoot again. He went over the side.

8

He found himself in an alley even darker and smellier than the one he and Wong had been in earlier. Wong was already near the end of it, and Fargo didn't think he had any choice other than to follow. Wherever Wong was going, he seemed to know the way. Fargo would just have to trust him.

There were rats in the alley, and Fargo saw their gleaming eyes. He was about to kick at one of them when a cat ran out of a cranny and jumped on it. The rat was nearly as big as the cat, and the two rolled over twice, squealing and hissing. By the time they came to a stop, the other rats had scuttled away under the buildings and into the walls, and there were three more cats on the attack. The remaining rat didn't stand a chance.

Fargo and Wong ran on through the twisting alleyways until Fargo figured that anyone looking for them would be hopelessly lost. His own sense of direction was practically unerring, but he thought that even he might have trouble finding his way out of the tangle of trails they'd followed.

Finally they came to a low door in the back of a house, and Wong pounded on it. Someone inside said something in a language that Fargo didn't understand. Wong replied, and the door was opened. Fargo and Wong ducked inside.

Fargo found himself in a small room lit by a couple of candles. There was a faintly sweet smell in the air. A small woman with dark hair stood before them, talking rapidly to Wong, gesturing at Fargo and at the door. She didn't seem glad to see them.

Wong tried to placate her, but she grew more and more agitated as they talked. Though the light was bad, Fargo could see that she was very beautiful, with delicate features and black eyes. She was wearing some kind of mannish shirt that concealed her curves, but for some reason Fargo was convinced that they would be well worth seeing.

Eventually the argument, or whatever it was, ended. Wong turned to Fargo and said, "This is my sister, Yee. She is angry because you and I have come to our home. She is afraid that the men who are chasing us will come here and cause trouble, maybe hurt someone."

Fargo asked how Yee could know that someone was chasing them.

"News travels very fast here," Wong said with a smile. "There are few secrets. When a white man comes into Chinatown, everyone knows." Wong's smile disappeared. His face turned grim. "Besides, as you saw, one of my people was killed."

"The law will take care of that," Fargo said, not believing a word of it.

Wong laughed bitterly. "The law does not care when a Chinaman dies. The law wants only to blame a Chinaman when a white man dies. As with that other friend of yours."

"You know about Nelson?"

Yee spoke for the first time, her voice soft and musical.

"As he said, Mr. Fargo, there are few secrets here. We know things about your town that no one would expect."

"It's not my town," Fargo said. "The longer I stay here, the less I like it. But I'd like to know how you find out so much. I can't seem to find out a thing."

"We know much because we are invisible," Wong said. "We work for the white men, but they do not see us. They talk in front of us as if we were not there. So we learn many things."

"What do you know about Taylor and Nelson?"

"Not so much. I have heard nothing about the man Nelson. I do know that he was not killed by one of my people. They had no reason to dislike him."

"And Taylor?"

"All I know is that Mr. King lied to you. I heard him talking to one of the other men about Mr. Taylor's murder. They did not seem displeased that it had occurred."

"But they didn't confess to it."

"No. But they were still talking when they walked away from me, so there may have been more said than I could hear."

"You said there were others who might know about Taylor. Who are they?"

"There is really only one," Wong said. "The man Mr. King was talking to."

"And who was that?"

"Deputy Marshal Sullivan," Wong said. "I think you know him."

"I know him, all right," Fargo said.

"He is a brutal man," Yee said. "He has killed more than one of us in that jail, but no one hears of it. The bodies disappear, and we do not know where they have gone. Their bones can never lie with those of their ancestors."

No one had to tell Fargo that Sullivan was brutal, and he thought he knew where the bodies had gone. Down at the bottom of some mineshaft, most likely.

Wong knew, too. He said, "No one will ever find them where Sullivan has thrown them. He is a devil."

"Maybe not a devil," Fargo said, "but he's not a man you'd want to let get the better of you."

"I think he got the better of your friend Taylor," Wong said. "Or someone did. Mr. King knows, I think."

Fargo wondered what he could do about that. He was wondering about something else, as well. He said to Wong, "How did you happen to be in that alley when I passed by?"

"I was trying to sneak to the Iron Dog. I was hoping to talk to you about Sullivan."

"What about those men? How did they find us?"

"I would also like to know the answer to that question," Wong said. "I can only believe that I was followed from the mine. Mr. King must not trust me. Now I cannot go back."

Yee spoke heatedly to him in their own language. After she was finished, Wong looked at Fargo apologetically.

"My sister is upset because we need the money. As bad as you might think we are being treated here, our situation was even worse in China."

"I might be able to help you out with the job part," Fargo said. "But first we'll have a little talk with Mr. King."

"I do not believe I want to see Mr. King again," Wong said.

"I want you to, though," Fargo told him. "Come to the Iron Dog in the morning."

Wong didn't look happy, but he agreed.

"Good," Fargo said. "I think I can find my own way back tonight, but you might want to go with me. I don't want anyone to think I killed that man."

"No one would think that," Wong said. "I wish, however, that we could find the two who did."

"We'll see what we can do," Fargo told him.

It was late when Fargo got back to the Iron Dog, and he had missed the excitement. He'd also missed the near-destruction of the saloon.

Marian summed up what had happened in three words: "Slade came back."

Her voice was tight and her face showed the strain of what had happened. So did the saloon. Slade had brought several men with him, enough, as it turned out, to break up most of the tables, shoot out the mirror behind the bar, break most of the liquor bottles, and put a hole in Ray's shoulder when he tried to fight back.

"He had himself a new shotgun," Ray said. "But he's not the one who shot me. That was some other son of a bitch."

About the only thing that hadn't been damaged was the piano. Glenn had watched the whole thing from his stool in front of it and hadn't suffered any more harm than the piano itself.

"Maybe they didn't want to kill me," he said. "They would have had to kill me to get at my piano."

"Maybe they just thought it sounded so bad already that they couldn't hurt it anymore," Fargo said. "What I want to know is how they knew I wasn't here."

"Could be they're not as afraid of you as you thought," Glenn said.

"Could be," Fargo agreed, but he didn't really think that was it.

There was something going on, something that he couldn't figure out, but it seemed to involve him and the men he'd brought to town. He looked around the ruins of the saloon. It could be put right with some hard work, but it would take a good bit of time, and there wouldn't be many customers. There were only three or four diehards sitting around now, and they'd soon be gone. The girls looked bedraggled and discouraged.

"Can you get more liquor in a hurry?" Fargo asked.

Marian nodded. "I had some squirreled away for an emergency. It's not the liquor I'm worried about."

"What about lumber?"

Fargo knew that in a mining camp, lumber was likely to be considered a luxury item, harder to get and more expensive than liquor.

"I know where I can get some if I pay enough for it. Why?"

"I think I know how we can fix things up pretty fast," Fargo said. "But it'll cost money."

"To hell with the money. I want to be back in business. Tomorrow."

"I don't know about that. How about tomorrow night."

"If that's the best you can do, I'll take it. But how can we get it done?"

"I'm not sure we can," Fargo said. "But we'll give it a try."

On his way back to Wong's place, Fargo stopped off at the Gypsy Queen. It was so crowded that he had trouble getting through the door. He recognized more than one face that belonged to regular customers at the Iron Dog. Most of them turned away when he glanced at them, though a few looked back boldly. He spotted Esmeralda near the bar and made his way over to her.

"I see business has picked up a lot," he said when he was near enough to be heard over the din of the crowd.

Esmeralda turned and gave him a pleased smile.

"It eez better than ever," she said, using her fake gypsy voice for the benefit of the customers. "And I have zee great Fargo to thank for it."

"Not to mention a man with a shotgun," Fargo said. "I thought Slade was out of the picture after our little talk."

"I do not know what you are talking about," Esmeralda said, taking his arm and drawing him away from the bar and through the crowd. They went into the little office where they'd had their first encounter and she said, "Now, what's this about Slade? I haven't seen him since before the last time you were in here."

"You're a beautiful woman, Esmeralda," Fargo said.

"I thank you for the compliment. I hope it's sincere."

"It's sincere enough, but you didn't let me finish. You're a beautiful woman, but you're a terrible liar."

"Liar? What the hell is that supposed to mean? Everything I said is the truth."

"Tonight Slade came back to the Iron Dog while I wasn't there. He and some other men shot the place up. There's not a customer left in it, and it's going to take days to set things right. Meanwhile, your business is booming."

"I've made improvements," Esmeralda said defensively. "I've done everything you suggested except get a piano, and I have one on the way from San Francisco right now. I don't need Slade anymore. I'm doing things the right way."

She was so convincing that Fargo almost believed her. But that didn't explain Slade.

Esmeralda must have seen that he wasn't satisfied. She said, "I don't know why Slade went back there, but it had nothing to do with me. You have to believe me, Fargo."

Her hands went to the buttons that ran down the back of her fancy dress, but she had made a mistake and forgotten to do something she'd done on their first visit to the room. She hadn't locked the door, which was flung open so hard that it slammed against the wall.

Marian stormed into the room, looking first at Esmeralda and then at Fargo.

"I didn't think I'd find you here," she said to him. "I thought more of you than that."

"I was just having a little talk with Esmeralda about Slade," Fargo said mildly. "Nothing to get excited about."

"Excited?" Marian yelled. "Who's excited, you son of a bitch? I'm not excited."

The last sentence was more of a scream than a yell, and Marian's face was so red that Fargo thought she might explode.

While all the yelling was going on, Esmeralda backed slowly toward the desk, keeping her eyes on Marian all the while. When she reached the desk, she ducked behind it and opened a drawer. Reaching inside, she pulled out a small pistol.

Marian was standing in front of Fargo, screaming in his face, but he could see Esmeralda over her shoulder.

He shoved Marian straight back. She hit the desk and tumbled across it. Her legs flew up, and she and Esmeralda fell to the floor in a tangled heap. The pistol landed a few feet away from them, and Fargo picked it up. By the time that he did, the women were going at each other, clawing, spitting, and pulling hair. The air was blue with their language.

Fargo considered wading into the fray and trying to pull them apart, but he decided that he'd just let them fight it out. No use for him to get a finger poked in his eye or a swift kick in some delicate part of his anatomy.

Esmeralda got to her feet, dragging Marian up by a handful of red hair. Marian reached out a hand and grabbed the front of Esmeralda's dress. She gave a strong pull, and the top of the dress ripped away, exposing a good deal of Esmeralda, much to the delight of the men who were now gathered in the doorway.

There was so much pushing and shoving going on for a good spot to view the proceedings that another fight erupted outside the office. Every time a man got in a good position to see, he was pulled away by someone bigger, stronger, or simply more eager to have a look. But nobody went easy, and soon there was a battle raging throughout the saloon. If Fargo didn't do something, the Gypsy Queen would be as big a wreck as the Iron Dog. There would be a certain justice in that, he thought, but he hated to see it happen. So he shoved a man out of his way, stepped through the door, and fired his Colt into the ceiling. He had to fire twice more before he had everyone's attention, and even then a few minor skirmishes continued to break out.

"All right," Fargo said. "That's enough fighting. All you men calm down, and I'll see to it that the women settle their differences."

"That's 'cause you got the gun," someone shouted. "We want to see, too!"

And he got his wish. Esmeralda and Marian hadn't stopped

at the sound of the gunshots, and they came careening out of the office locked in a grotesque embrace.

Marian had her fingers embedded in Esmeralda's long black hair and appeared to be trying to rip it out by the roots. For her part, Esmeralda was hanging onto Marian's throat with both hands, though she wasn't able to get a grip powerful enough to choke her.

People moved out of the way, and the women danced clumsily across the floor of the saloon. Both their dresses were torn, and there was a good deal of flesh exposed. Nobody seemed to mind. They all just wanted a better look.

Marian backed into a chair and fell, pulling Esmeralda down on top of her. Esmeralda took advantage of the chance to get a better grip on Marian's throat, and Fargo thought he'd better take a hand, after all. He didn't want anybody to get killed, and he was working for Marian. It would look bad if he stood by and let his employer be choked to death.

He went over to the women and took hold of Esmeralda's shoulders. He tried pulling her up, but she refused to let go of Marian. Fargo released her shoulders and walked around in front of her so that he could get hold of her wrists. He took them and squeezed, looking into Esmeralda's mad eyes.

"Let her go," he said. "I don't want to break your arms, but I will if I have to. Let her go."

Esmeralda spit in his face.

Fargo sighed and squeezed until he had almost crushed the bones in her wrists. Then he jerked her hands apart. They came off Marian's throat, and Fargo threw Esmeralda aside. One of her customers caught her, but as soon as she could get away from him, she stalked back to her office and slammed the door shut.

Fargo helped Marian sit up and asked if she was all right.

"No thanks to you, you traitorous bastard," she said, rubbing her throat with one hand and pushing Fargo with the other. "Get away from me. I'm going to kill that bitch."

Fargo helped her to her feet. He said, "You're not going to kill anybody, but we'll both go and have a little talk with her."

"We tried that already. Now we'll kill her."

"No," Fargo said. "We won't."

He got a firm grip on Marian's arm, and they went back to

the office. Fargo tapped on the door. There was no answer. He tapped again a little more forcefully.

"Go away," Esmeralda said from inside. "I will not open zee door."

Fargo lifted his right leg and kicked the door, hard, right where the lock joined the frame. The door popped open, and Fargo went in, closely followed by Marian. Fargo closed the door behind them. It swung back open, so he put the chair against it.

"Now, then," he said. "We're going to finish our little discussion. First, Esmeralda, you're going to tell Marian why I came here."

Esmeralda pouted and held her torn dress in front of her as if she were the most modest woman in the Nevada Territory.

"Tell her," Fargo said.

"Oh, very well. You came here to accuse me of sending Slade to wreck the Iron Dog. But I didn't do it."

"I saw what you were doing," Marian said. "You whore."

Esmeralda dropped the part of the dress she was holding and came at Marian. This time Fargo stepped between them in time to prevent another fight from breaking out.

"Esmeralda and I were just talking," he said. "I don't know what you think you saw, but that's all that was going on."

Marian gave him a look that said she didn't believe a word of it.

"And if there *was* anything else going on, that's my business," Fargo said. "And Esmeralda's."

Marian didn't like that any more than anything else she'd heard, but she held her peace. Esmeralda smiled faintly.

"Fine," Marian said after a while. "Let's say it's like that. But that doesn't excuse what she had Slade do to my saloon."

"You must not have been listening," Esmeralda said. "I told you that I didn't have him do it. I haven't even seen him for days."

"I was listening," Marian said. "I just don't believe you."

"I do," Fargo said, putting up a hand to forestall any more angry words from Marian. "Slade wasn't delivering a message to you this time."

"Then who was he delivering it to?" Marian asked.

"Me," Fargo said.

9

Fargo sat in the Iron Dog, sitting at one of the few undamaged tables, drinking a cup of coffee. It wasn't much after six o'clock, and Marian wasn't an early riser. Wong was, however. Old Pete, the swamper, came to tell Fargo that there was a Chinaman at the back door.

"Says you told him to come," Pete said. "I couldn't chase him off."

"It's a good thing you didn't," Fargo said. "He's going to help us set this place to rights."

"Take a hell of a Chinaman to do that," Pete said, spitting a long brown stream in the general direction of a spittoon near the bar.

He didn't seem to care whether he hit it or not, and neither did Fargo. After all, Pete was the one who had to clean it up.

"I can't tell him to come in here," Pete said, wiping his mouth on his dirty shirt sleeve. "Miss Marian don't allow that kind of thing."

"I'll talk to him," Fargo said.

He hadn't gotten back to Wong's last night because of the fracas at the Gypsy Queen, but he could ask Wong this morning about his plan for the saloon.

Fargo set his coffee cup on the table and went to the door. Wong was standing in the alley, a round cap in his hands. His long pigtail hung down almost to his waist.

Be a bad thing to have something like that attached to you in a fight, Fargo thought.

"Good morning, Wong," he said.

"Good morning, boss," Wong said. "Boss say Wong come to saloon in morning, and Wong here. What boss want of Wong?"

"First, I want you to drop the funny talk," Fargo said. "You can talk better English than I do. So do it."

Wong ducked his head in a kind of bow and looked up at Fargo.

"If you say so. Most white people don't like it when I speak good English."

"I'm not most white people. Do you know any good carpenters, men who could use a day's wages?"

"Wong know lotsa men . . ." He stopped when he noticed the way Fargo was looking at him. "What I mean to say is that I know quite a few men who need the wages. Some of them are good with their hands."

"Good. Get them over here. I have some work for them. And for you, too."

"What kind of work?"

"This place got shot up last night. I need some men who can rebuild some tables, fix some walls, things like that. Carpenters, like I said."

"I'll bring the men," Wong said. "What about supplies?"

"I'll take care of that," Fargo told him.

The hardest part had been waking up Marian. Fargo didn't do it. He sent one of the girls. Marian finally came out, looking sluggish.

"This better be good," she said.

Fargo told her his plan and said, "I'll need some money for lumber. You said you could get some."

"Just hold on a minute. Chinamen? In the Iron Dog?"

"What difference does it make to you who does the work, as long as it gets done?"

Marian thought about it. She said, "None, I guess, not as long as they do it right."

Fargo had a feeling it would be done right. It had better be if the second half of his plan was going to be put into effect. He said, "Good. Now tell me where I can pick up that lumber."

It was surprising what twenty fairly skilled men could do in one day. By late afternoon, the Iron Dog was in better shape than it had been before Slade's visit, and customers

75

began to drift back in. In fact, some of them had come earlier, just to watch Wong and his crew at work as they repaired the chairs, fixed the tables, patched the walls, cleaned the floors, and removed the glass and litter that Pete hadn't bothered with earlier in the day. They weren't able to fix the mirror, but they managed to patch enough of it together that it somehow looked almost whole.

"Who'd've thought a Chinaman could do work like that?" someone said to Fargo.

"Give a man a chance, and there's no telling what he can do," Fargo said.

Marian was pleased with what she saw, and she congratulated Fargo for thinking of using Wong. She also offered a halfhearted apology for her behavior of the previous night. While she was in a contrite mood, or as close to it as she ever got, Fargo told her what else he wanted her to do.

"Hire a Chinaman?" she said. "Why?"

"Because he's smart, he's a good worker, and he'll help you make money."

All those things must have sounded good to Marian, but she still wasn't convinced.

"Tell me how," she said.

Fargo told her his idea. She didn't like it.

"This is a saloon," she said, "not some fancy restaurant. I don't need a cook."

"You already have a cook," Fargo pointed out, which was true in a sense.

When Pete wasn't cleaning up the place, he could sometimes be persuaded to fix a meal for Marian or one of the girls. The food wasn't very good, but it was edible. Most of the time, anyway.

"And you have a kitchen," Fargo went on. "You don't have to serve the customers if you don't want to, but everyone would be a lot happier with someone who can really cook."

"How do you know the Chinaman can cook?"

"His name's Wong."

"Fine. Wong. How do you know Wong can cook?"

"That's what he's been doing at the Silver King. But I don't think he should go back."

"Why not? Did he get fired?"

"Not exactly," Fargo said. "It's a long story. The point is that we know Wong can cook. He'd be a big help around here, and if you decided later that you wanted to serve food to some of your special customers, you'd even make some more money. Think it over."

"All right," she said, an hour or so later. "I've thought it over. I'll hire your Chinaman."

"He's not my Chinaman," Fargo said. "And his name is Wong. I hope you're going to get that right from now on."

Something in the way he said it must have convinced Marian. She said, "Don't worry. I won't have any more trouble with the name. Do you want to tell him he's hired?"

All the workers had finished, been paid, and gone home. The Iron Dog was filled with customers, and Glenn was beating on his sour-sounding piano.

"I'll tell him," Fargo said. "I'll go now if you don't think Slade will be back."

"Two nights in a row?" Marian said, arching an eyebrow. "Surely not."

"If he shows up, send somebody for Marshal Sullivan."

Marian laughed. "That man's a bigger criminal than Slade ever was."

Fargo said he didn't doubt it, but that Sullivan was the law.

"The law works in its own way here in Virginia City," Marian said. "I thought you'd have figured that out by now, considering your little rumpus with Sullivan."

"I guess you're right," Fargo said. "But if a man can't trust the law, who can he trust?"

"Nobody," Marian said. "Hell of a note, isn't it."

Fargo agreed that it was.

There was no trouble on the way to Wong's place, no mysterious men with guns lurking in alleys, no policemen arresting him for murder. Just the ordinary crowds on an ordinary night.

Things were a little different in the Chinese section. People regarded Fargo with suspicion and got out of his way quickly as he walked through the narrow streets. He thought they might be blaming him for the death of the man the previous evening. Or maybe they just treated all white men like that.

He found Wong's place without too much trouble, and Yee opened the door. Fargo noticed again how pretty she was, and he wondered if he'd ever get a chance to find out what she was wearing beneath her all-too-concealing clothing.

"Good evening," Yee said. "What brings you to our humble home, Mr. Fargo?"

"I'm looking for Wong. It's about a job."

"Another job? For all the men?"

"Nothing like that. Marian wants him to cook at the Iron Dog."

"Wait here," Yee said, and left Fargo standing there at the door.

There was the smell of cooking in the house, but Fargo couldn't identify the odors. He had no idea what kind of food Wong fixed for his own family, or whether someone else was the cook.

Yee came back with Wong. He seemed glad to see Fargo.

"Yee says you have news."

Fargo explained about the job at the Iron Dog.

"I am a good cook," Wong said. "Miss Marian will be glad she has hired me."

"I hope so. King didn't seem too impressed."

Fargo hadn't mentioned King's displeasure to Marian. He hadn't thought it would be a good idea.

"I did not like Mr. King," Wong said. "So I did not do my best."

"You mean you might even have done a bad job on purpose?"

"The men did not treat me well, except for your friend Mr. Taylor. Mr. King was even worse. He paid me, but he did not pay me fairly. I felt cheated."

"Marian won't cheat you."

"I did not think she would. She was very generous with the men today. They were glad to work for her."

"You'll be glad, too," Fargo promised. "You start in the morning."

"I will be there," Wong said. "Thank you, Mr. Fargo."

"Just Fargo will do."

"I don't think so. It would not be proper. What does not bother you would bother others."

"We'll see about that," Fargo said.

The next day, Wong was at work early, ready to cook for anyone who wanted to eat. Fargo ordered ham and eggs, and Wong cooked them up expertly. Fargo didn't think anyone would have room for complaint.

When he was finished, Fargo took his coffee out into the saloon to sit and think things over. He considered everything that had happened, starting with the murders of Taylor and Nelson. He'd told Utley and the others that he'd try to do something, but so far he hadn't done a thing except visit the Silver King.

The reason for that was simple: He didn't have any place to begin, other than the fact that Taylor had worked at the mine. As far as Fargo knew, the only connection between the two dead men was their trip to Virginia City. There was nothing in that to cause anyone to kill them. He'd have to try to find out more about both of them.

And then there was Slade. Fargo was sure that Slade had shot up the Iron Dog to get back at Fargo for humiliating him at their first encounter. But how could Slade have been so sure that Fargo wouldn't stop him again? Had he known that Fargo wasn't in the saloon? And if he'd known that, how had he found it out? It was possible that he'd been watching the place, or having someone do it, but Fargo thought he would have noticed something like that.

There were some other things that bothered Fargo, too, things that he couldn't quite put his finger on, things he'd heard or seen that hadn't meant much at the time, but that were somehow nagging at him, just out of reach of his memory. Maybe they'd come to him later.

One thing he wanted to do was have another talk with Sam King. The mine owner was in cahoots with Sullivan, or at least Fargo suspected that he was. Wong had seen the two talking about something, maybe about Taylor. But Fargo didn't know of any reason why either man would have killed

Taylor. The truth of it was, he didn't know a whole hell of a lot about anything.

He took his cup back to the kitchen and left it with Wong. Then he went out into the saloon and told Glenn that he was leaving for a while.

"You can let Marian know, if she asks," Fargo said.

"Where you headed?" Glenn wanted to know.

"Up to the Silver King," Fargo said.

"You know those people?"

"Not as well as I hope to," Fargo said.

There were a couple of reasons Fargo wanted to visit the mine again. If Wong was telling the truth, and Fargo didn't have any reason to doubt him, then King and Sullivan knew each other. And someone in King's employ liked to use a shotgun. Whoever it was had been standing inside the office building when Fargo and King had their little encounter, as if he had a reason to keep out of sight. Maybe he didn't want Fargo to recognize him. If that was the case, it could have been Slade, who was known to like a shotgun. If Slade was in King's employ, that would mean that more than likely Slade, Sullivan, and King were all somehow tied together.

And for that matter, it wouldn't be too surprising if Slade was working for King and Esmeralda at the same time. Men like Slade took their jobs where they could find them. Or it could mean that there was some connection between Esmeralda and King. Fargo didn't know of one, but that didn't mean anything. There was a lot he didn't know about the things that were going on in Virginia City.

He walked up to the mine, breathing in the cool morning air and listening to the sound of the stamp mills pounding. Every now and then there would be a dull rumble under the ground as if the earth were belching, but the ground hardly shook. Nobody seemed to notice. Everyone in Virginia City was used to the noise and the tremors.

Nobody paid any attention to Fargo, either, as far as he could tell. He tried to spot a watcher, maybe someone who'd picked him up when he left the Iron Dog, but he was sure no one had even noticed his departure.

When Fargo reached the Silver King, there was no one

around. The miners were all underground, and King was nowhere in sight. There were men working in the stamp mill, but it was making so much noise and they were so busy at their jobs that none of them noticed Fargo. He decided to have a look at what was going on.

The stamp mill's purpose was to extract the ore from the rock, and it was built on several levels, the top one being the rock breaker. From there the material went to a crusher, and then to the pans before going through a separator and into an agitator with a series of screens. The silver was obtained at the end by an amalgamation process. Fargo didn't understand the procedure, but he knew that it had been used in California for gold mining. In fact, the first stamp mills in Virginia City had been brought in pieces over the mountains from California and reassembled.

Fargo went inside the mill. The air was filled with rock dust, and the noise was much louder than it had been outside, a constant cracking and rattling. A couple of men were standing over by the agitator, and Fargo went over to talk to them. The men didn't hear his approach, and he tapped one of them on the shoulder. The man looked around, seeming a bit startled that someone had sneaked up on him.

"I'm looking for a man named Taylor," he said. "Jim Taylor."

He had to raise his voice to be heard at all, and the man looked at him as if he'd asked for the Queen of England.

"Never heard of him," he said.

He was tall and bearded. There was rock dust in the beard, and Fargo could see the black dust covering his clothes, clinging to the sweaty patches.

"I heard he was working here for Sam King," Fargo said.

The man shook his head and said, "You must have the wrong place, friend. Nobody by that name around here."

Fargo started to say more, but the man turned away, giving Fargo his broad back. His companion, who hadn't said a word, shook his head and turned away as well.

Fargo wasn't going to let them off that easily. He put his hand on the bearded man's shoulder and said, "Hold on a minute. I'm not through talking to you."

The man turned back, frowning. But the frown turned to a grin, showing bad teeth through the middle of his beard.

"Oh, yes, you are," he said.

Fargo felt the man standing behind him a moment before he heard him, and he started to turn. He was much too late. Something hit him very hard in the back of the head, and that was the last thing he knew for a while.

10

Fargo felt himself being lifted. It made him a little dizzy and a little queasy, but he tried to open his eyes. He succeeded, but he couldn't see anything. It was too dark.

Fargo's head hurt and throbbed. Being dropped into some kind of container didn't make it feel any better. He lay in a heap on the cold metal floor, wishing he could do something about his situation. But he was practically unable to move.

"Should've just killed the son of a bitch up there where we found him," a man said.

"Couldn't do that, Rascoe. We don't want the men to think there's something funny going on around here," another man said.

Fargo thought he recognized the voice. Slade.

"You don't think seeing a man hit in the head and hauled off won't strike them as being a little strange?" Rascoe said.

"Mr. King told them he was an intruder, somebody trying to steal the mine's secrets."

"What secrets?"

"Mr. King didn't say. Let them guess. That's always the best way."

"That other fella guessed," Rascoe said.

"Yeah, and you know what happened to him. Some of the rest of 'em do, too, and when somebody comes snooping around asking about him, he disappears. They'll be wondering what it's all about, but they'll keep their mouths shut. They don't want to disappear, you can bet."

"Speaking of disappearing," Rascoe said, "ain't it time we started this fella on his last long ride?"

"Might as well," Slade agreed.

Fargo had figured out that he was somewhere down in the

depths of the Silver King. That's why there was hardly any light. Slade and his friend Rascoe might have a candle or lantern, but there was no other illumination. And the container in which Fargo now found himself was a mine cart. He was about to be sent somewhere from which Slade and Rascoe thought there would be no coming back.

"We oughta shoot him," Rascoe said. "Be certain about it."

"Can't do it," Slade said. "Much as I'd like to. But we're in an old part of the mine that was built before they figured out the square sets. This timbering's barely holding up the top. If we shot the bastard, the whole mountain might fall in on us."

"Goddamn," Rascoe said. "Then let's get out of here. Help me give this thing a push."

Fargo tried to sit up. He thought his head might fall off if he did. As he was struggling, he heard a squealing noise, and the cart started to move. It went only a few inches at first, and he could hear Rascoe and Slade grunting as they gave it another shove.

This time, the cart started to move quickly, rumbling over the rails.

"So long, Fargo," Slade said. "If you come back, you can tell us how deep that hole is at the end of the line. I'm guessing a mile."

Fargo could barely make out the last remark because the cart had already traveled too far for him to hear clearly. The thunder of the wheels reverberated from the walls, and he was in complete darkness.

He finally managed to sit up, gripping the edge of the cart with his hands and pulling himself up so that he could see over the edge. Except that he couldn't see a thing.

The cart was picking up speed with every passing second. Fargo didn't much like the idea of jumping out of it, and he wasn't even sure he could. But he liked the idea of falling into a mile-deep hole a lot less.

He pulled himself erect and let himself fall over the side of the cart. He threw his hands up over his head to protect it and landed hard on his shoulder. He rolled along the side of the track, bouncing off the wall now and then and scraping several square inches of skin off his hands, arms, face, and back.

Eventually he came to a stop. He didn't feel like moving,

much less standing up and going back up the tracks after Slade and Rascoe. But he knew that he had to. If he didn't, he'd be down there in the dungeon-like darkness with no chance of a light and no idea how to get out. He didn't let himself think of how it would be if he didn't catch up with Slade. The rails might lead him out, or they might not. He couldn't count on it. He *had* to catch up.

Behind him the noise of the cart suddenly stopped. He guessed it had come to the end of the track, but he couldn't hear it falling, and he didn't intend to stick around to see if he could hear it land. He started off after Slade, every inch of him twinging with pain.

After he'd gone a few steps, he reached down to see if by some stroke of luck Slade had left him the Colt. The holster was empty. Slade hadn't forgotten anything, except that he should have hit Fargo one more time, just to be sure he wouldn't wake up. For that matter, maybe he'd hoped Fargo would wake up, at just about the time the cart sailed off the track and into whatever deep pit was waiting for it.

Fargo followed the tracks. After only a minute or so, his long legs were stretching out into their usual loping stride, or as close to it as he could come on the uneven ground. He hoped that Slade and Rascoe were taking their time. After all, they didn't have any reason to think that someone would be coming up behind them.

Before too long, he thought he saw a glimmer of light up ahead, and then he was sure he did. He also heard voices. He stepped up his pace, being careful not to make any noise. No use in giving a warning.

He put out a hand and touched a wall. It was cool, which he hoped meant they weren't too far down. He knew that in some of the deeper mine tunnels there was steaming water right behind the walls, and more than one miner had struck the wall with a pick only to find himself parboiled by the powerful stream of water that hissed out over him.

Everything was going well until Fargo stepped on a rock that turned under his foot. He caught himself on the wall before he fell, but the rock rattled away and struck the rail. Fargo held himself absolutely still and waited to see what would happen.

"What the hell was that?" Rascoe asked.

"Loose rock probably fell out of the wall," Slade said. "It happens now and then."

"I don't like it," Rascoe said.

Fargo could tell from the sound of his voice that he hadn't moved. If anything, his voice was a bit clearer than it had been. He was probably looking back down the tunnel.

"You think it's a ghost?" Slade said. There was a hint of derision in his voice. " 'Cause there's nothing else back there 'cept for Fargo's ghost."

Slade chuckled at his little joke, but Rascoe wasn't amused.

"Bullshit on ghosts," he said. "Ghosts don't make noises like that."

"No," Slade said, "they don't. That's because there's no such thing as ghosts. And no such thing as Fargo now, either. He's so far down in the ground that he's lying about as near to Hell as you can get without going there. Come to think of it, he's probably done that, too."

"I think we should have a look," Rascoe said. "I know I heard something."

"A loose rock. That's all. But if you want to go back and see, go ahead. I'll wait right here for you."

"You're the one oughta go. You're the one that Mr. King pays to do the dirty work. I don't make enough to tangle with the likes of that Fargo, don't matter if he's dead or alive."

"You're the one worried about the noise. Either go yourself, or shut your trap about it."

The next thing that Rascoe said wasn't clear to Fargo. It sounded as if the man might be muttering.

"Go on," Slade said, "and stop the whining. Or we can leave. Take your pick."

Fargo hoped that Rascoe would be as lazy as Slade and let it slide, but Rascoe couldn't quite do it. Fargo heard him say, "I'm going. But you wait right here."

"I ain't going anywhere," Slade said. "Get on with it."

Fargo could hear him coming. Rascoe wasn't making any attempt to hide his approach. It could have been that he hoped whoever was there would hear him and be afraid. But fear wasn't an option for the Trailsman. He was looking forward to meeting Rascoe alone and in the dark.

He felt around on the floor and found a fragment of rock about the size of his fist. That would do just fine, he thought. He'd give Mr. Rascoe a headache the size of the one Rascoe and Slade had given him.

Seeing the light approaching a turn in the tunnel, Fargo hid himself as well as he could behind an outcropping of rock. Rascoe was mumbling to himself as he walked along, and Fargo could tell he wasn't happy with his partner.

"Bastard Slade should be the one doing this," Rascoe said. "He's the one responsible. But I know who'd catch hell if something went wrong, and it wouldn't be him. No, hell, no. It'd be old George Rascoe, that's who it'd be."

Fargo almost felt sorry for him. Almost, but not quite. He pressed himself against the wall of the tunnel, trying to become a part of the rock, and waited.

Rascoe went right by Fargo without a glance in the Trailsman's direction. The light from a tall candle he was carrying bounced shadows off the wall. Fargo could make out enough to realize that Rascoe was one of the men who'd been in the saloon with Slade when Fargo had first met him. Rascoe had been carrying a club then, but he didn't have one now.

Fargo let him get about six feet away and then whispered, "Rascoe."

He had to give Rascoe credit. The man was quicker than Fargo had thought, and quieter. He turned without a sound, fast as a striking rattler, bringing up his pistol and thumbing back the hammer.

Unfortunately for Rascoe, however, Fargo was even faster, not to mention mad as hell about the way he'd been treated. He didn't let Rascoe get the pistol level. He stepped forward and smashed him in the mouth with the rock.

Rascoe might have wanted to cry out, but he didn't get a chance. The rock crushed his lips and knocked out most of his front teeth. He bowed his head as if to lament his loss, and Fargo hit him in the back of the head with the rock, in just about the same spot where Fargo had been hit. Rascoe crumpled silently to the ground, dropping both his pistol and his candle.

The candle hit the floor, and Fargo grabbed it before it went out. He held it steady for a second or two to let the faltering flame right itself. When it was burning brightly, Fargo picked up the pistol.

He was glad Rascoe hadn't fired it. Even if he'd missed, he might have started a cave-in that would have covered them both. Fargo almost imagined that he could hear the old timbers cracking above him.

The pistol was an old Colt's Dragoon, and Fargo hefted it. It would work just fine as a club if he had to use it. He slipped it in his holster and bent down to Rascoe. It was a little tricky to arrange his hand and fingers so that he was holding the candle in an upright position, but Fargo managed it. Then he moved back into the darkness a little way up the tunnel to see what Slade would do.

He didn't have to wait long. After a couple of minutes, Slade called down the tunnel.

"Rascoe? What's keeping you?"

Slade's voice echoed off the rock walls. Fargo didn't answer. Neither did Rascoe, which wasn't surprising, considering his state of consciousness, or lack of it.

"Rascoe, you better not be messing with me," Slade said. "I'd just as soon leave you down there to rot."

Another few seconds of silence passed. Fargo wondered if Slade would come check on Rascoe or if he'd just leave. Leaving would be the smart thing, but nobody ever said that people like Slade were smart. Clever maybe, but not smart.

"I'm coming to get you, Rascoe," Slade said, confirming Fargo's suspicions about his lack of intelligence. "If you're screwing with me, it'll be the sorriest day of your whole sorry life."

Maybe Slade wasn't stupid, Fargo thought. Maybe he was just curious, wondering if Rascoe would have the nerve to try to play a trick on him.

Slade didn't come down the tunnel as noisily as Rascoe had. He didn't make a sound. In fact, if it hadn't been for the steady advancement of the light, Fargo would never have known that Slade was on his way.

Fargo wasn't behind the outcropping this time. He'd gotten into the shadow of one of the timbers that was shoring up the ceiling, and the rough square of wood was hiding him from Slade's view.

Slade stopped when he came within sight of Rascoe, and he proved his cleverness by not coming a single step farther. He'd stopped about a yard in front of the timber where Fargo was hiding.

"Son of a bitch," Slade said, and Fargo could imagine him taking in the sight of Rascoe lying there, his head caved in and the candle clutched in his outstretched hand.

"Couldn't be a ghost did that," Slade said. "No such thing as a ghost. And Fargo's long gone. What the hell?"

He took a tentative step forward, holding his own candle high so that he could see more of the area, and Fargo stepped out from behind the timber, jamming the pistol barrel into Slade's side.

"Hello, Slade," Fargo said. "Where's your shotgun?"

"You turd," Slade said, lowering the candle. "I'm not stupid enough to carry a gun like that down here. But I don't need it for you. I don't know how you got out of that cart, but I'll kill you anyway."

"Like you killed Taylor and Nelson?"

"Who?"

"You know who."

"Nope. Can't say as I do. I don't know anybody by those names, and I never did."

Fargo couldn't tell if Slade was lying or not. Maybe Taylor wasn't who Rascoe and Slade had been talking about. It didn't matter. Fargo said, "How did you know I wouldn't be in the saloon when you came back?"

Slade smiled crookedly. "Just lucky, I guess."

Fargo wanted to pull the trigger of the Colt and make sure Slade never smiled again, but he restrained himself.

"Esmeralda's changed the way she does business, and I don't think she's the one who sent you to the Iron Dog a second time. Why'd you come?"

"To show you that you can't get the best of me," Slade said.

"I'm not the one with the pistol stuck in his side," Fargo pointed out.

"You wouldn't dare pull that trigger. You'd cause a cave-in."

"Maybe," Fargo said. "Maybe not. I think there's enough fat on you to muffle the noise pretty well, don't you?"

Obviously Slade hadn't thought about that. He tried to move away, but Fargo was right on him, keeping the pistol barrel pressed hard into his flesh.

"Do that again," Fargo said, "and I'll kill you. I might even enjoy it."

Slade held still after that, and Fargo lifted his pistol, which he stuck in his belt. Fargo's Colt was in Slade's belt, so Fargo took that, too, and holstered it.

"Did you kill Rascoe?" Slade asked, not sounding as if he cared one way or the other.

"I just hit him," Fargo said. "Like you hit me."

"That wasn't me," Slade said, passing the blame. "That was Rascoe."

"I don't care who it was," Fargo said. "You're the one who was going to send me to the bottom of the mine. Maybe that's where you should go. I still think you killed Nelson and Taylor. Why did King have you do it?"

"Mr. King doesn't tell me what to do."

That was the first obvious lie Slade had told. Fargo thumbed back the hammer of the Colt.

"Jesus, be careful," Slade said. "You might shoot me by accident."

"It won't be an accident," Fargo said.

"Don't even joke about that. You know you couldn't find your way out of here without me."

"I'll just follow the rails," Fargo said. "They'll take me out sooner or later."

"No they won't. They wind around and then stop. After that, there's too many tunnels for you ever to get out. You'd wander around in here till you died."

Fargo didn't believe it. But he didn't want to spend any more time underground than he had to. He said, "All right. You can take me out. We'll leave Rascoe here with his candle."

"You're a hard man, Fargo," Slade said.

"Sometimes that's the only way. Let's get out of here."

Fargo reached for Slade's candle, and Slade stuck it in his face.

11

Even before the hot wax struck his cheek, Fargo knew he'd made a mistake. He'd been aware of the risk of standing so close to Slade, but he'd taken the chance in the hope that Slade would be too flabbergasted at seeing Fargo alive to try anything.

Too bad it hadn't worked out that way.

Fargo jerked his head backward, and Slade hit Fargo's wrist with the side of his hand, knocking the pistol aside. Instead of going for his own gun, Slade put a knee into Fargo's crotch.

Fargo doubled over and dropped the candle, which sparkled when it hit the rock floor and then went out. The one in Rascoe's hand still burned.

Slade laced his fingers together and brought his fists down like a hammer on the back of Fargo's already throbbing head. Fargo hit the floor like a sack of sand, and Slade tried to kick him in the face.

At the last second, Fargo's reflexes took over, and he managed to catch hold of Slade's boot just before it landed. Fargo held the boot steady with both hands while Slade struggled to get it free. He could smell the stink of Slade's sweat. He twisted, but Slade didn't fall.

Slade hopped around on one foot until Fargo's grip loosened. Then he yanked his captive foot away and reeled backward. He stumbled on the rails and almost fell again, but somehow he retained his balance.

Fargo slumped down, the pain in his head threatening to crack his skull. Slade drew his pistol, but he caught himself before he pulled the trigger. Instead of firing, he holstered the gun and reached down to pluck the candle from Rascoe's fingers.

91

"So long, Fargo," he said, and walked away.

Fargo stayed where he was, half-lying, half-sitting. His head was pulsing so hard that he felt as if his eyeballs might pop out, and he put up his hands to press them back in. After what seemed like an eternity, the pulsing finally stopped, though his head still hurt.

When he opened his eyes, he couldn't see a thing.

Slade was long gone, and the mine was utterly dark.

Fargo stayed where he was for a while. He'd heard stories about men who'd been lost in mines for days and how they were struck blind by the sun when they finally found their way out. He'd also heard about rivers in caves so deep and dark that the fish in the rivers were blind. He wondered how long it would take a man to go blind if he never saw that light, not that it would matter to Fargo. He'd starve to death long before that could happen.

He didn't intend to die underground, though. He was going to get out of the mine and take care of Slade.

But first he had to get some light. He started feeling around on the rough rock floor for the candle that Slade had dropped. It took him quite a while, but he finally located it. Now all he needed was a lucifer to get it lit.

He wondered if Rascoe carried matches on him. He was feeling his way toward him when he heard Rascoe stirring.

Fargo stopped where he was and listened. If Rascoe was awake, he'd be easier to find, though he was a much bigger object than the candle had been.

After a few minutes, Rascoe was fully awake and calling out for Slade. His voice sounded lispy and mushy because he'd lost so many teeth.

"Slade, goddamn you, where are you?"

There was, naturally, no answer.

"Son of a goddamn' bitch. Son of a fucking goddamn' bitch. He's left me here to die in the dark."

Fargo heard Rascoe struggle to his feet.

"Shit," Rascoe said. "I don't know which way to go."

He kicked around until he found the rails.

"I can follow 'em just fine," he said, but he didn't sound

too confident to Fargo. "I'll be able to tell if the slant is up or down. Damn' right."

Fargo hadn't become disoriented, so he knew which way to go. He waited to see if Rascoe guessed right.

He did. Maybe he really could tell the slant of the tunnel, or maybe he was just lucky. It wasn't all that obvious to Fargo, who waited until Rascoe had gone past him before speaking.

"Got a match?" he said.

Rascoe must have jumped, though Fargo couldn't see it. Rocks clattered under his feet.

"Shit!" he said. "Who's that?"

"It's me. Fargo."

"Slade left you, too, huh?"

"Yeah. He's not a very considerate fella."

"He ain't the one broke out all my teeth," Rascoe said.

Fargo imagined that Rascoe was listening carefully, hoping to locate Fargo by his voice and maybe do him some harm. So Fargo moved silently a few feet closer to him.

"Fargo?" Rascoe said. "You still there?"

Fargo didn't answer.

"I got a match," Rascoe said. "I got a couple of 'em. You got a candle?"

Getting the matches might be a problem, Fargo realized. Rascoe would no doubt rather have the candle himself than give up the matches. Fargo didn't think they'd be able to work out an amicable trade. Too bad that Rascoe had come to.

Too bad for Rascoe, that is.

Fargo got behind him and tapped him with the butt of the Dragoon. Rascoe fell in a heap without making a sound. He might not ever make another one, but that wasn't Fargo's concern. He ran his hands over Rascoe's clothing and located the lucifers in a pocket. In a couple of seconds, he had the candle lit. He thought he'd never been so glad to see shadows dancing on a wall before. Now all he had to do was find his way out of the mine.

He took more than one wrong turn and ran into more than one dead end, but he went more or less steadily uphill. After quite a while, he saw the bright daylight outside the entrance. He stopped where he was so he could take stock of things. He had no idea what might be waiting for him out there, but he had plenty of guns. The question was whether he was in any condition to use them. He was scraped and bruised. His head hurt. He was covered in rock dust and dirt. His face was probably burned.

None of that really mattered, however. What mattered was getting out of there and finding Slade. He went on toward the entrance.

The sunlight outside was nearly blinding after all his time in the dark, so Fargo stood just inside the entrance until his eyes adjusted to the illumination. When he thought he was ready, he stepped out, pistol in hand.

There was no one there, and no sign of the Silver King mine. He'd been transported somewhere else. He should have figured that. He hadn't heard any mining activity, and Slade wouldn't have wanted to dump him where there could be any witnesses.

Fargo looked around and tried to figure out exactly where he was. It was clear that nobody had been around this abandoned mine for a while. There were a couple of dilapidated shacks that showed no signs of habitation. There was no stamp mill. This was someone's worthless claim, left there for anyone to use for whatever purpose was fitting, including disposing of dead bodies.

Wondering how long it would take him to find the road, Fargo started walking. Each step sent a jolt of pain up to his head, which seemed to be getting worse instead of better with the passage of time. He almost stumbled when he started down the slope toward where he hoped to find the road. He wondered if he could make it back to town, even if he could find the way, which was seeming less and less likely.

His vision blurred. He wiped at his eyes, thinking that perhaps it was the sunlight.

It wasn't. His feet got tangled up again, and this time he did stumble, falling into an awkward trot downhill as he tried to keep his balance. He couldn't. He fell, sliding on his back and winding up halfway behind a large rock. He raised his head, which seemed very heavy, to look around. He couldn't see a thing, so he closed his eyes and gave in to the dark.

*   *   *

There was a strangely familiar scent in the air. Fargo couldn't quite identify it, though he knew he's smelled it before.

He opened his eyes. He was lying in a dark room on a small bunk, covered with a sheet. There was no one else there. He sniffed the air again, and this time he recognized the smell. It was the odor of cooking and clean laundry that he'd first noticed in Wong's house, but this time there was something else, a faint medicinal odor.

Fargo sat up and touched his fingers to the back of his head, which for some reason didn't seem to be hurting anymore. He felt a bandage that was greasy with some kind of ointment. He also noticed that he didn't have any clothes on. He felt clean, as if he'd had a bath. He was wondering how he'd gotten undressed, bathed, and into a strange bed, when the door opened and Wong was silhouetted by the light.

"Good evening, Mr. Fargo," Wong said. "I hope you're feeling better."

"Just Fargo. And I'm feeling better, all right, better than I have any right to. How come I'm in your house?"

"I didn't know where else to take you. Also, you needed help, and this seemed like the right place to bring you. My sister is a healer of sorts."

Fargo remembered Wong's sister. "Yee," he said.

"Yes. She knows quite a lot about herbs and other cures. She has put an ointment on your head. She also gave you a special tea to drink."

"Thanks," Fargo said. "My head was thumping like somebody was using it for a drum, but it's stopped now. How did you happen to find me?"

"I was at the Silver King. I felt bad about not having told Mr. King that I would no longer be in his employ, and I thought I would let him know. I believed I was doing the right thing, but I was wrong. He was very angry with me. His face got red, and I thought he was going to hurt me, but while I was talking to him, Mr. Slade came into the office. Mr. King forgot all about me then, and they began discussing you. As I have told you, no one sees a Chinaman or believes he knows what is going on around him, so I listened without shame. Mr. Slade said that he had left you for dead in the old Dutchman's mine. I knew that it was not far from the Silver

King. After a few minutes, Mr. King noticed that I was still there and dismissed me. I immediately went to look for you. When I found you, I went for help. Then I returned and brought you here."

"I owe you for that," Fargo said.

"You owe me nothing," Wong said. "It is I who owe you. You have saved me from Mr. King's employ and given me a new and better way to earn money. You have helped my countrymen find work as well."

"I have to get back to the Iron Dog," Fargo said. "Marian will wonder where I am."

"I told her that you are safe. She did not ask questions."

That was like Marian, Fargo thought. She didn't pry. He appreciated that quality in a woman.

"Yee will bring soup in a while," Wong said. "You should eat it all. It will give you strength. But now, rest."

That sounded like a good idea to Fargo. He lay back on the thin pillow and closed his eyes.

Fargo didn't know how much time had passed when the door opened again. He sat up as Yee came into the room and set something on a low table. Then she closed the door and lit a lamp that sat on the table. Fargo saw that a bowl of steaming liquid sat beside the lamp.

"I see that you are awake," Yee said.

In the lamplight Fargo noticed again how beautiful she was. It was a look that was different from what he was accustomed to, but her black hair and eyes set off the fragile beauty in a way that he found irresistible.

"I appreciate what you've done for me," he said. "I know you don't want me here."

"What happened previously was not your fault, as Wong has explained to me. I am sorry that I was angry."

"You don't have to apologize. After all, you've practically saved my life."

"No, I have not done that, but I have tried to make you better. Your head has been hit very hard, and any movement is dangerous for a person in that condition. You were in no danger as long as you were lying still, but exertion was not good for you. That is why you fell. But after some rest and food, you will be much better."

"Speaking of food," Fargo said, "I see you brought some."

"Yes. I will help you eat."

Yee turned to get the bowl. Fargo was about to tell her that he didn't need any help when he realized that she would be sitting on the bed beside him, spooning soup into his mouth. He thought that might be very pleasant, so he said nothing about his ability to feed himself. Instead he said, "Wong told me that there would be medicine in the soup."

"Yes," Yee said, bringing the bowl to the bed. "It will make you feel better, though you still should not exert yourself."

Fargo moved over, and Yee sat on the edge of the bed. The savory smell of the soup made Fargo's mouth water.

"What's in that soup?" he asked.

"It is an old family recipe," Yee said, not exactly answering the question. "Here."

Yee dipped a wooden spoon into the bowl and held it out for Fargo to taste. He opened his mouth, and Yee put the spoon to his lips. The soup was hot and spicy. It tasted like nothing Fargo had ever eaten before, but he liked it a lot.

"I think I could get used to that," he said.

"You do not have to get used to it. But you must eat it all."

"With you helping, that should be no trouble," Fargo said, looking Yee in the eyes.

It was hard to tell in the lamplight, but Fargo thought that Yee blushed. He smiled and continued to eat the soup as she spooned it up for him.

When he had eaten all the soup, Yee put the bowl back on the table. Then she turned to Fargo. She said, "You are a strange one, Mr. Fargo. You are big and tough, but at the same time you seem to care about what happens to me and Wong. I have never met a foreign devil quite like you."

"I'm not exactly foreign," Fargo said, "and I'm sure not a devil. I guess you know I'm just a man if you helped Wong take my clothes off. And especially if you helped give me a bath."

Once again, Yee appeared to blush.

"You are a man," she said. "But not *just* a man, not judging from what I saw."

"And what exactly was that?"

Yee shook her head. The lamplight shone in her dark hair.

"I cannot say," she told him.

"Maybe I could show you something that would loosen your tongue."

"And just what would you show me?"

"Something that I think you've already seen once before, except that it's going to be a little longer and stronger than it was a while back."

That wasn't an exaggeration. Just thinking about Yee had caused Fargo's shaft to grow hard and erect, making a little tent of the covers.

Yee looked at the bed. She smiled and walked over to the door, where she turned a key in the lock.

"There are different kinds of exertion," she said. "Some of them do not hurt a person in your condition at all. In fact, some can be very restorative."

"What kinds are those?" Fargo asked, but he had an idea that he already knew the answer. He hoped so, anyway.

"You will see," Yee said, and she began to take off her clothes.

Fargo watched her disrobe. She was smaller than most women he had known, but everything about her was perfectly proportioned. Her breasts were small and firm, like apples, and the tips were stony hard with anticipation. Her legs were short but slender. Her waist was narrow, and her hips flared invitingly. There was only one surprising thing: She had no hair at the junction of her perfectly formed thighs. Her skin appeared to Fargo to be as smooth as a baby's.

"You seem surprised," she said, standing there boldly and letting his eyes rove over her body.

"It's just that I never knew anyone so . . . slick," Fargo said.

Yee grinned when she understood his meaning.

"Ah. I have been shaving there ever since I came to this place. It is much easier to keep clean that way."

She walked seductively across the room and tossed back the blanket that had covered Fargo. She looked down at his imposing erection with admiration. If anything, it had grown somewhat larger during the second or two it had taken her to cross the room.

"You are so large," she said, "and I am so small. Do you think you will hurt me?"

Fargo didn't think so. In fact, he figured it was just about impossible. There was one thing that worried him, however.

"This is a mighty small house," he said. "What if someone hears us?"

Yee smiled. "I do not think we have to worry. My family likes to mind its own business, and even if someone should cry out, I can tell them that it was simply a part of the healing process."

And that might even be true, Fargo thought. After all, there was generally nothing that made him feel better than a good romp in the bed with a beautiful woman, and this one was truly beautiful. His steely shaft twitched in anticipation.

"Ah," Yee said. "You seem eager to begin."

"And what about you?" Fargo asked.

He reached out and slipped his hand between her legs. She rubbed herself against his sideways palm, and he felt that she was at least as ready as he was. Maybe even more ready. He caressed the pubic mound with his thumb. It wasn't as smooth as it had looked, but it was certainly smoother than any Fargo had ever encountered. He moved his hand back and forth between her legs, and Yee gasped with pleasure.

"You had better stop," she said, breathily. "If you do not, I will surely achieve my pleasure before you find your own."

"And what's wrong with that?" Fargo asked. "Besides, I have a feeling you can achieve it a lot more than once."

"But how can that be?"

"You'll see," Fargo said, continuing to rub.

She helped by pressing herself down to increase the pressure and within a few seconds she had closed her eyes and crossed her hands over her breasts, squeezing them to her. Her breathing grew more and more rapid, and soon her breath was coming in short huffs and puffs.

"*Ohh. Ahh. Ohh. Ahh,*" she moaned.

Fargo sat up straighter in the bed and pulled her closer with his free hand. Then he gently moved her crossed arms and put his mouth to her right breast.

"*Ahhhhhhhhh*," Yee said, as Fargo ran his tongue around the nipple, tasting its hardness and then closing his mouth around it and sucking it in, along with some of the tender skin surrounding it.

"*Ohhhhhhhh*," Yee sighed.

Suddenly she gave an abrupt jerk, her whole body stiffening. She reached out and clasped her hands on Fargo's shoulders, holding to him tightly as one tremor after another ran through her body. She said something soft and sibilant in her own language, and while Fargo didn't understand a word of it, he had a pretty good idea of what she meant.

After a while she collapsed into Fargo's arms. He was very conscious of his stiff pole, which was caught between his belly and her own. It was so hot there that it was as if both of them had fever.

Yee recovered quickly and lifted her head to smile at Fargo.

"That was the best thing that has happened to me in this country," she declared.

"Then I have some good news for you," Fargo told her.

"What is that?"

"The best is yet to come," he said, and his erection gave a twitch.

"Oh. Could it be possible? I do not see how."

"You will," Fargo promised, raising her up so that the tip of his shaft was touching the hot opening his hand had so recently fondled.

Yee moved her hips enticingly, teasing the tip by allowing it between her lips for a short time before it slipped out again. Soon she was moving faster as she discovered that indeed she could experience the same pleasure more than once. Her opening expanded and grew hotter and slicker with each movement she made until finally she could stand it no longer.

"I want you, Fargo," she said. "Please. Put it in me!"

"Sure I won't hurt you?" Fargo joked.

"Oh . . . oh! Please! Now! Now!"

Fargo put his hands on her hips and held her still while he located exactly the right spot. Then he pushed her slowly down, impaling her on his erection to about half its length.

"*Eeeeeeee*," she said, her hips churning.

She rose up off Fargo until only the tip of his penis remained in her. For a moment she hung there as if suspended. Then she plunged herself down, forcing the rock-hard shaft into herself up to its full length.

She hardly paused before rising again, then sliding back down. She was moving so fast that Fargo was almost immediately at the peak of his pleasure. Yee's black hair whipped from side to side, and her eyes were closed in a transport of ecstasy.

Fargo felt the muscles knotting in his legs and a powerful force began to gather, starting almost down at his toes. He matched the fury of Yee's movements with a powerful thrust or two of his own. She bounced up and almost lost him, but at the last moment she slipped back down again.

Finally Fargo could not hold back. He felt a volcanic eruption shoot out of him in one great burst that was soon followed by another, and then another.

At the same time, Yee reached her own climax. She bit her lip to hold back a scream, and the tremors that had wracked her earlier were nothing compared to what happened now. It was as if she were seized by a demon spirit that shook her from head to toe. Her muscles tightened in a grip that milked Fargo of his essence.

Eventually they were quiet. Yee lay on Fargo's chest, breathing softly, his left arm around her back.

"I never knew," she said. "I never knew."

"We foreign devils may not be healers, but we have our own secrets," Fargo said.

"I believe you do," Yee said. "I have never felt like that before. Never."

"You can again, though. Just about any time you want to."

"Now?" Yee said.

"Well, that might be a little tricky," Fargo told her.

She rolled to one side of him in the narrow bed and took his penis in her hand.

"You forget that I know the arts of healing," she said, moving her hand up and down its length.

Sure enough, Fargo started to grow hard almost at once.

"You certainly do," he said. "You can even raise the dead."

"It wasn't dead. It was only sleeping."

"Yeah, I guess you're right. It's sure awake now."

"And I know just what to do with it," Yee said. "Maybe even something you have never done before."

"You'll have to prove that to me," Fargo told her.

So she did.

12

Fargo walked back to the Iron Dog with Wong the next morning.

"I hope you rested well, Mr. Fargo," Wong said as they left the house. "My sister said that she took good care of you."

Fargo didn't detect any hint of irony in Wong's tone, and his face was bland. But then so were the faces of the others they passed on the street. The Chinese had learned how to prepare a face for the faces they met in the streets of Virginia City, and it was a face that revealed nothing.

"It's just plain Fargo," Fargo said. "How many times do I have to remind you of that? You save a man's life, and you don't have to call him *mister.* You don't have to, anyway."

"It is better that I do," Wong said.

Fargo decided not to pursue that topic any further. Wong seemed determined to call him *mister,* no matter what. So Fargo said, "Your sister is an expert healer. I feel better now than I did before I got hauled down that mine shaft."

Fargo wasn't exaggerating. He couldn't say whether it was the lovemaking or the soup or the tea that he didn't remember drinking or even the salve on his head, but something had made him feel very good, much better than a man in his condition should feel. He hoped it wasn't just an illusion.

They made their way through the busy streets. Even early in the morning the mining town was going strong. There were times that things slowed down a little, but there was always something going on. The whole place stirred with life and energy.

But the truth was that Fargo didn't really like it. Oh, he could live there for a while, and he planned to stay until he learned who'd killed Nelson and Taylor, but he preferred living outside of cities and towns, under an open sky, where there wasn't so much noise and bustle all the time. He was beginning to feel cooped up, like some kind of caged bird. He didn't want to stay in his cage so long that he forgot how to fly.

Fargo and Wong went into the saloon through the back door, and Wong got ready to fix breakfast. Glenn came into the kitchen as soon as Wong started banging the pans around and lighting the stove.

"Hey, Fargo," Glenn said. "I thought maybe you'd lit out for the tall and uncut when you didn't come back. I bet Marian is fit to be tied."

"She knows where I was," Fargo said. "Wong told her."

"Oh," Glenn said. "I guess that's all right, then. And where the hell were you, anyhow?"

"Out," Fargo said. "Don't scramble my eggs too hard, Wong."

Glenn didn't seem to notice the change of direction the conversation had taken, and he continued to talk to Fargo about where he might or might not have been. Fargo just ignored him until Wong brought eggs, ham, and biscuits to the table. After that both men were too busy eating to talk.

Fargo was surprised that his appetite was so good. He'd thought that after all that had happened, he might not feel like eating again for a while. But it turned out that he was ravenous. He finished his first helping and asked Wong for another. There must be something to that Chinese healing, for sure.

After he finally finished eating, Fargo went out into the saloon to look things over. Slade hadn't paid any more visits, and everything looked good. Ray was already behind the bar, and he waved when he saw Fargo.

It was several hours before Marian emerged. She seemed glad to see Fargo, but more because he stood for protection against Slade than because he was her lover. Which was fine with Fargo. That was the way he preferred it.

"You were right about Wong," Marian said. "He's a good cook, and I think I might let a few special customers eat in the kitchen. Provided they can pay, of course."

"Of course," Fargo said. "You're here to make money."

"That's right. And there's plenty to be made." Marian

smiled at the thought, but her smile turned to a frown. "Unless Slade comes back when you aren't here."

"I'm thinking about what to do with Mr. Slade," Fargo said.

"I hope that when you make a decision, it involves something bad. For him, I mean."

"You can count on it," Fargo said.

The rest of the morning went by calmly, but just before noon two things happened that upset the tranquility.

One wasn't exactly unexpected. Someone robbed the stage again.

The man who brought the story in said that it was the same as always.

"Took the silver and robbed the passengers," he said. "Real polite about it, is what I hear. Nobody got hurt."

"They never do," someone observed, "but it's just a matter of time until it happens again."

"Hell, I guess the miners don't care," the first man said. "They're making so much money that losing a little silver now and then doesn't bother them."

Fargo walked over to where the men were standing at the bar and joined the conversation.

"Nobody likes to lose money," he said. "Did Sam King have any silver on that stage?"

"Sam? Hell, I doubt it. Far as I know, that son of a bitch ain't never lost a dime. He's almighty lucky if you ask me, but then a man that finds a vein of silver like he's got, has been blessed with luck for a long time."

Fargo said he guessed the man was right and went over to listen to Glenn play an out-of-tune waltz. He was still standing by the piano when Deputy Marshal Sullivan pushed through the batwing doors, shoving them so hard that they popped back against the walls.

People sitting near the entrance either got up and moved away or huddled over their drinks as if hoping that they could shrink down so small that Sullivan wouldn't see them.

But Sullivan didn't care about them at all. He was looking straight at Fargo.

"God save all here," he said, though he didn't take his eyes off Fargo.

Fargo nodded but didn't speak. Sullivan smiled widely.

"Cat got your tongue, Fargo?" he asked. "Don't you want to know why I'm paying you a visit on this beautiful day when I could be outside taking the fresh air?"

"I don't much care why you're here, Marshal," Fargo said. "I'd like it a lot better if you'd leave."

Sullivan looked around the room. No one there except Fargo and Marian would meet his gaze.

"Brave words," Sullivan said. "Mighty brave. We'll see later if you have the gumption to back 'em up, we will. And how about you, Miss Marian? Aren't you the least bit curious about my handsome presence here today?"

Marian looked him up and down. Then she said, "Handsome, Sullivan? I've seen old dogs with worms and the mange that were more handsome than you."

Sullivan's smile faltered, but for so short a time that no one noticed it but Fargo, who also noticed the red that began to rise up Sullivan's neck. However, Sullivan's voice was level when he spoke again.

"Well, well. They say a sharp tongue is the only edged tool that gets keener the more it's used." He shook his head. "But enough of this shilly-shallying. Nobody seems interested in why I'm here, but I'm going to tell you anyway."

"Spit it out, then," Marian said. "The sooner you say it, the sooner you'll get out of my saloon."

"I'm afraid it's bad news," Sullivan said.

"I've known that all along," Marian told him. "Nothing else could put you in such a good mood."

"Ah, Miss Marian, you wrong me. But be that as it may, here's what I have to say. Mr. Fargo, you're under arrest again."

Fargo hadn't thought that Sullivan would try again. He said, "What's the charge?"

"It seems," Sullivan said, "that you've killed another one of your friends."

Fargo was surprised, and he didn't mind showing it.

"Which one?" he asked.

"A Mr. Edwards," Sullivan said. "The barber. Not a finer one in Virginia City."

Sullivan was laying it on thick for the crowd, but Fargo

doubted that Sullivan had ever met Edwards. Probably hadn't ever seen him.

"So if you'll just come along with me, Fargo," Sullivan said, "I'll see to it that justice is done."

Fargo had a pretty good idea of the kind of justice that was in store for him if he went with Sullivan, having had a small sample of it already. So he said, "Sorry, Sullivan. I think I'll have to turn down your invitation."

"Ah, but that's the beauty of being a deputy marshal," Sullivan said. "No one can turn you down."

"I can," Fargo said.

"He sure can," Ray said.

He was holding the shotgun, and it was pointed right at Sullivan's midsection.

"I see what you mean," Sullivan said.

He looked around the room, meeting Marian's eyes with a smile. The look he gave Fargo was a little less friendly, but Fargo wasn't bothered.

"If that's the way it is, I suppose I'll be leaving," Sullivan said. "A good morning to all of you."

He turned to leave, swaggering across the floor. Ray tracked him with the shotgun.

When Sullivan reached the batwings, he reached out as if to open them, but instead his right hand went to his pistol. He pulled it out, whirled and fired.

The bullet hit Ray squarely in the middle of his chest. There was a look of great surprise in the bartender's eyes, and he was dead before he fell.

As he fell, however, his finger tightened on the trigger of the shotgun, loosing a blast of buckshot that swept the center of the room, spraying into tables, breaking glasses, and ripping through the clothes and flesh of several customers.

Fargo drew his Colt and was about to sent a bullet after Sullivan, but it was too late. The deputy marshal had hit the floor rolling after shooting Ray, and he was already out in the street. Fargo didn't want to take the chance of hitting someone who had no part in the fracas.

"That bastard," Marian said. "He's killed Ray. He'll be back with more men, Fargo. You'd better get out of here."

Wong stuck his head out of the kitchen door and beckoned to Fargo.

"You come with me," he said. "I can take you where the marshal cannot follow."

Fargo didn't like the idea of running, but it didn't seem like he had much choice. If Sullivan came back with more men and guns, he'd shoot up the saloon and everyone in it. There were already wounded men at three different tables, and Ray was lying dead behind the bar.

"Don't just stand there, Fargo," Marian said. "Go with Wong."

Fargo went. He and Wong were out the back and into the alley in only a couple of seconds, but there were already men coming toward them from both ends. Sullivan had been prepared.

Across the alley there was a stairway leading up to a lawyer's office on the second floor of a dry-goods store.

"We go up," Wong said, running toward the stairs with Fargo right behind.

When Wong reached the landing, he jumped lightly to the railing and pulled himself up onto the roof as easily is if it were something he did every day. Fargo, being taller and heavier, didn't have quite so easy a time, but he was encouraged to hurry by the bullets being fired in his direction from the alley. They chipped the railing and the roof, and sent splinters flying in all directions. Sullivan didn't seem to care if he took Fargo dead or alive.

Fargo rolled over onto the roof on his back, and Wong reached down a hand to pull him to his feet.

"This way," Wong said, and started across the roof.

Fargo followed, and they jumped from roof to roof, headed for the Chinese section of town. Sullivan's men were following in the street, firing and hoping for a lucky shot. Fargo wasn't really worried. It was hard enough to shoot a man while you were standing still. To hit what you were shooting at while you were running was next to impossible. And in fact, none of the bullets even came close.

"We will lose them easily," Wong said, starting down a stairway that led to a narrow, darkly shaded alley.

They left the alley and soon were lost in the crowds that

seemed to open in front of them and close in behind them like water.

"Where are we going?" Fargo asked, knowing that Wong wasn't headed in the direction of his house. Which was a shame, since Fargo wouldn't have minded seeing Yee again.

"I know a place," was all Wong said.

Before long they had left the town by a route that Fargo didn't know. Wong led him along a twisting path up the mountain. He was moving fast, and soon Fargo was feeling a little short of breath, though Wong didn't seem bothered at all. The terrain looked familiar, and Fargo asked where they were.

"Near the mine where they left you for dead," Wong said. "No one will think to look for you there."

Sure enough Fargo saw the tumbledown shacks through the trees, though he and Wong were not coming at them from the road. When they arrived, Wong said, "This accommodation is not as nice as the one you had at the Iron Dog, but I will bring some bedding for you later. You can stay here, and they will not find you."

"What about you?" Fargo asked. "Sullivan will find a way to get the truth out of you, either that or he'll kill you."

"Not me," Wong said. "Miss Marian will protect me."

Fargo knew she'd try, but he didn't think she could do it. He told Wong that.

"I believe she can," he said. "If it is necessary. You forget that to men like Sullivan, all Chinamen look alike. He will not know who was running across the rooftops with you. His men will not be able to describe who was with you other than to say that it was a Chinaman. There are many in Virginia City who fit that description."

Fargo had to admit that Wong had a point.

"I'll stay here, then," Fargo said. "Until I figure out what's going on. That might be a long time, considering I haven't got much to go on."

"I'm sure you will find the answer," Wong said.

Fargo wished he were as confident as Wong sounded. He said, "I need you to do one more favor for me."

"You need only to ask," Wong said, so Fargo did.

=== 13 ===

Waymon Carter and Lane Utley showed up at the shack later that afternoon.

"We got the word from that Chinaman of yours that you were hiding out here," Utley said. "What the hell is happening, Fargo?"

Utley's skin was already beginning to lose some of the dark coloring it had gotten when he was a farmer. As it lightened, it seemed to be growing closer to his bones, and his face was almost skull-like.

"First of all," Fargo said, "he's not *my* Chinaman. His name is Wong, and he's his own man. And I don't know what's happening any more than you do. I was hoping you could tell me."

"All we know is that Edwards is dead," Waymon Carter said.

There was something in Carter's eyes that hadn't been there before, Fargo noticed. It was a sheen of fear. He and Utley were the only ones left of the men who'd come to Virginia City with Fargo, and Carter looked as if he might be afraid his own time was coming.

"How was he killed?" Fargo asked.

"You sure you don't know?" Utley said. "Word is that you're the one that killed him."

Fargo looked around the little room where they were. There was no furniture, and the floor was nothing but hard-packed dirt. Light leaked in through the roof, and dust motes spun in the sunbeams. Fargo stood with his back against a wall that was so rickety that a good strong wind would blow it over in a winter storm. All in all, the shack was the kind of place where a hunted killer might wind up, Fargo thought. He couldn't blame Utley too much for the way he was thinking.

"I didn't kill him," Fargo said. "You should know that."

"Hell, I don't think you killed him," Carter said, "but somebody sure as God did. When we asked you to find out who killed Nelson and Taylor, we were hoping you might do it before somebody else got murdered."

Fargo felt bad about not having done exactly that. But he hadn't had anything to go on. He still didn't have anything.

"There's got to be something tying the bunch of you together," he said. "And somebody's got it in for me, too. But I can't figure out what or who."

"Neither can we," Utley said, "mainly because there's not anything. Edwards cut our hair, like he cut Taylor's, but nobody kills you because you give a bad haircut."

"Aw, they weren't that bad," Carter said, and Utley gave him a withering look.

"What about the Silver King?" Fargo asked. "Everything seems to go back to that place somehow. They sure didn't take to me asking questions the first time I was there."

He didn't mention the second time. He'd get to that later.

"Hell, nobody wants somebody coming around asking questions about his claim," Utley replied. "Me and Carter would get mighty upset if somebody came poking around the Missouri Beauty. That's the name of our place. We'd feel the same, and we aren't even digging out any silver the way they are at the King."

"It won't be long," Carter said, though Fargo could tell his heart wasn't in it. "We're going to hit a vein any day now."

"The thing is," Utley went on as if Carter hadn't spoken, "if some stranger comes poking around, he's gonna be in trouble, no matter where. You can't lay it all off on the Silver King if they didn't like you messing in their business."

Fargo knew that Utley could be right, but there seemed to him to be something wrong at the Silver King. He just couldn't quite put his finger on it. Of course there were the obvious things, like Slade being there. And Slade had implied that he'd had something to do with at least one disappearance before Fargo had showed up.

But Fargo still hadn't figured out Slade's place in the whole

111

scheme of things. He knew Slade stood with King, of course, and maybe even did his dirty work, but what about Esmeralda? Was Slade still working with her? And what about Sullivan? Wong had seen him and King together, talking about Taylor. It was all a big jumble, but he knew that somehow it all fit together. Unfortunately Fargo still couldn't arrange the pieces the right way.

"They're gonna get us all," Carter said, shaking his head. "And we don't even know why. If I have to die, I'd like to know why. That's not asking too much, is it?"

Neither Fargo nor Utley bothered to answer him. Even Carter probably knew how ridiculous his question sounded.

"So what are you gonna do about it, Fargo?" Utley said after a while.

"I wish I could tell you," Fargo said. Then he remembered something. "You still haven't told me how Edwards died."

"Shot in the back," Carter said. "He left the barber shop last night and was locking the door. Damn lot of good that did him. He died right there in front of the place, with probably twenty people close by, and not a single one of them could say who shot him."

"Or wouldn't," Utley said. "You know, Fargo, they've been after you from what I hear. I wonder why they just haven't shot you."

"They decided there was a better way," Fargo said, and told them about being carried down into the mine.

"So that's why you don't like King," Utley said. "I can't say as I blame you, but I might've done the same in his place. You say that Slade fella mentioned something about you stealing secrets?"

"That's right," Fargo said. "But I don't think he really believed it."

"He could have, though. It's like I say, nobody likes people who come poking around."

"Maybe," Fargo said.

But he couldn't help thinking there was more to it than that.

For a long time after Utley and Carter left, Fargo sat on the dirt floor and leaned back against the boards of the weather-beaten wall, thinking. He didn't come to any real conclusions, and sometime after dark, Wong showed up with some biscuits, ham, and soup.

"Yee sent the soup," Wong told Fargo. "She says that it will do you good, though you are already well and strong again."

Fargo thought there were other things he'd rather have from Yee, but it wouldn't be right to talk about them to her brother. He thanked Wong for the food and asked about what had gone on in the Iron Dog that day.

"Nothing of importance," Wong said. "Everyone wants to know where you are, but I have told no one, not even Miss Marian. She was angry at first, but then she understood."

"I'm glad somebody understands something around here," Fargo said, settling down to eat.

When he was finished, he felt better about things. Maybe it was something in the soup. He thought Yee should sell it to the miners. She could make a lot of money.

"She is not interested in making money that way," Wong said when Fargo mentioned it. "Her healing is a secret. If people come to her, she helps. But she does not do it for money."

Fargo thought that was noble of her, but not very sensible. He decided not to say that to Wong, who might not understand.

"What are you going to do?" Wong asked, gathering up the bowl and plates.

"I don't know exactly," Fargo said, "but I have to go back to town. I guess all I can do is keep pushing and see who pushes back. Maybe sooner or later, somebody will tell me something or I'll figure something out."

"You could also get killed," Wong said. "Sullivan did not return to the Iron Dog, but he is looking for you all over town. His men were in the Chinese section today. They were not careful of the way they searched."

"I'm sorry to hear that," Fargo said. "I seem to be causing you a lot of trouble."

"It is nothing," Wong said. "We are glad to help you. Those men would find some excuse to harass us if you had never come here."

There was just enough truth in that to give Fargo a bit of comfort. He said, "I hope when this is over, they'll leave you alone."

"I know you will make it so," Wong said.

"You have a hell of a lot more faith in me than I do."

Wong smiled. "You will triumph in the end. You will see."

"I hope you're right. So far, things don't seem to be going my way."

"Things change," Wong said.

"Yeah," Fargo agreed. "And it can't happen too soon to suit me."

It was time to start pushing. Fargo decided to start with Esmeralda. She was a lot better looking than either Sullivan or Slade, and there was something funny about the way Slade had appeared at the Iron Dog when Fargo was gone. He'd understood that she wouldn't be sending Slade out any more, and yet he'd nearly destroyed Marian's place.

At first Fargo had thought that Slade had done it as a warning from King, but now he wasn't so sure. Maybe Esmeralda hadn't been as sincere as she'd seemed.

Well, there was one thing she was sincere about, Fargo thought with a grin, remembering what had happened on the couch in her little office. There wasn't any doubt about how much she'd enjoyed that. So had he. But that didn't mean she was undyingly loyal to him or that she wouldn't lie to him if it would serve her purposes.

Fargo went outside. The night air was crisp, and the sky was clear. The moon was round and silver, and the stars glittered in profusion. Fargo could have been a million miles from anywhere.

But then he heard the distant rumble of the stamp mills, and he knew that he wasn't far away from the so-called civilized world at all. Not far enough, at any rate. He started back into town.

The Gypsy Queen was livelier than it was when Fargo saw it last, and there had been a number of improvements. The whole place looked cleaner, even the girls. There was a piano, and it was in tune. Fargo wondered how Esmeralda had gotten a piano so quickly, and how she'd found someone to play it so well. She'd spent a lot of money, and the crowd was considerably larger than it had been on Fargo's last visit.

Fargo thought there were plenty of miners in Virginia City

to support two first-class saloons, and he didn't see why there had to be a fight about it. But then, there were quite a few things he didn't understand about the way business was done in the mining town.

Esmeralda saw him when he entered. She had just come out of her office, and she crossed the room to greet him.

"Fargo!" she said. "What a pleasure it ees to see you again."

The accent was back, but Fargo figured Esmeralda had to keep up appearances. It wouldn't do for people to get the idea that the Gypsy Queen was run by a woman who was no more of a gypsy than they were.

Her black hair glistened, and her smile was wide. Her eyes sparkled, but there was something in them that Fargo didn't trust. He was almost certain that she wasn't as pleased to see him as she pretended to be.

"Hello, Emeralda," he said. "Your business has improved."

"I took your advice," she said, putting an arm around his waist to draw him to the bar. "Your first drink is on the house."

Fargo ordered a beer. The bartender drew it up and slid it down the bar. Fargo caught it and took a swallow.

"Not bad," he said. "I hope you're not watering the whiskey anymore."

Esmeralda laughed, but there was a hollow ring to it.

"Of course not," she said. "But then I never did. That was just a vicious rumor started by your friend at the Iron Dog."

Fargo didn't think it was a rumor. He wondered what was bothering Esmeralda. He didn't expect her to drag him immediately into the office for another round on the couch, but he'd thought she'd be at least moderately glad to see him. Unless, of course, she hadn't kept up her end of the bargain. That would mean she was the one who'd sent Slade back to the Iron Dog and that the destruction hadn't been a message to Fargo. Or that someone was trying to kill two birds with one stone. Fargo decided he'd find out. He was tired of all the complications.

He set the beer mug on the bar and said, "You lied to me."

Esmeralda looked around the room to see if anyone had heard him, but everyone was too absorbed in conversation, gambling, or listening to the piano to have paid any attention to Fargo's brief speech.

"I never lie," Esmeralda said, turning back to Fargo. "I don't even know what you're talking about."

"You sent Slade back to the Iron Dog."

Esmeralda put a hand on the bar and considered him. After a while she said, "I never told you that I wouldn't."

Fargo thought back to their conversation. Sure enough, he couldn't remember her having said a thing about not sending Slade back. She had sort of implied it, and Fargo had wanted to believe that she wouldn't, but she had made no promises.

"I apologize," Fargo said. "You're right. You didn't lie. You're just treacherous. I should never have trusted you. But then you know how to get men to trust you, don't you."

Esmeralda flashed him a brilliant smile.

"And were you disappointed?"

"Not at all. Were you?"

"No. That is the good part. It was far better than I expected."

"Then maybe we should do it again," Fargo said.

Esmeralda's smile slipped, but she caught herself and renewed it.

"I would like nothing better, but we cannot."

"I'm sorry to hear you say that. I thought we might be able to go in your office and talk this over like friends, maybe have us a little fun at the same time. But I see we can't. That's all right. We're going to have the little talk anyway."

"But we cannot. I have business to attend to, and I cannot desert my customers."

"You didn't seem to mind deserting them the other night."

"That was different," Esmeralda told him.

"I'm sorry, but I don't see it that way," Fargo said. "It might have wound up as something else, but it started out as business. And this is business, too. Let's go."

Esmeralda looked over his shoulder at the bartender and raised her eyebrows. Fargo whipped out his Colt and turned around before the bartender could make a move.

"Just stay where you are," Fargo said. "Esmeralda and I are going to her office for a little talk. She'll be just fine, so I

116

wouldn't come barging in if I were you. If anybody does that, she might get hurt. Understand?"

The bartender nodded.

"Good. Now, then, Esmeralda, let's me and you go on back there and talk."

Esmeralda didn't move. Fargo said, "If you don't get started, I might have to do something with this gun. Shoot the piano, maybe, so it'll play out of tune like the one at the Iron Dog. Or put a few bullets into that mirror behind the bar. You might not be able to find anybody to fix it up until you get a new one, and that'd be a real shame."

"Bastard," Esmeralda said.

"I sure wish you wouldn't talk like that. It makes me think less of you."

"I'll just bet it does, you long-legged country clodhopper. All right. Let's go."

She swept by him and headed for the office. Fargo holstered his gun and followed, glad to let her take the lead. He had a feeling there was a good reason she didn't want him back there, and he was interested in finding out what it was. You never could tell with a woman like her. Maybe she had a man in there. Hell, maybe she had two.

She opened the door with her right hand and stepped to the side. With her right hand still on the knob, she gestured to someone in the room with her left hand, and then stepped through the doorway. Her body had partially concealed the gesture, but Fargo had seen it. He figured there was someone in there, all right, and he drew the Colt as he entered.

But there was no one there except Esmeralda. Maybe he'd misjudged her, after all.

She turned to him and smiled. She said, "Why don't you close the door, Fargo, so we can have our little talk in private."

"Want me to lock it?" he asked.

"Why don't you do that," Esmeralda said. "You never know what might happen in here."

Fargo stuck the Colt in the holster and closed the door, turning the key in the lock. When he turned back to face Esmeralda, Slade was standing up from behind the couch. He was holding his favorite weapon, a shotgun, and it was pointing Fargo's way.

117

Esmeralda smiled. It wasn't a pleasant smile. It was predatory and cruel. Fargo didn't like it at all.

"Like I said," Esmeralda told Fargo, "you never know what might happen in here. I forgot to mention that Slade had come by. He was going to pay another visit to the Iron Dog while you were gone."

Fargo wondered how they always knew when he was gone. Sullivan was the source this time, most likely, though there were no guarantees.

"Looks like we meet again, Fargo," Slade said. "To tell you the truth, I never thought you'd get out of that mine."

"What about your friend Rascoe," Fargo said. "How's he doing?"

"I wouldn't know. I haven't seen him lately. I guess he's the one that didn't get out. I owe you for that."

"No need to feel obligated," Fargo said. "I was glad to do it."

"I didn't mean it that way, you son of a bitch."

"Sorry. I guess I misunderstood. Did you go looking for him?"

"That ain't none of your business," Slade said, but Fargo knew the answer.

Slade didn't give a damn about Rascoe or anybody other than himself. He was just using Rascoe as part of his justification for killing Fargo, which Fargo knew he was planning to do. Not that he needed any justification. He had Esmeralda to encourage him.

"Go ahead," she said to Slade. "Cut him in two with that scattergun."

Slade smiled and held the shotgun steady.

"I'm ready to do it. You sure you want to clean up in here when he's dead?"

It was a good question, Fargo thought. A man with a bullet in him might bleed on the floor, but the shotgun in close quarters could make a real mess. It would put hair and meat on the walls.

Esmeralda considered the situation, then said, "I hadn't thought about that. We'll have to do it outside."

Fargo couldn't see why everybody wanted him dead. He hadn't killed anybody, not in Virginia City, that is. And he didn't know anything that anybody wouldn't want him to know. He was just doing his job in the Iron Dog Saloon, not bothering anybody who didn't bother him first. It was all tied up somehow with Taylor and Nelson and Edwards, and maybe even the Silver King, but it didn't look like he was going to live long enough to find out how all the pieces fit together. Not if Esmeralda and Slade had their way.

But then Fargo had no intention of letting them have their way. He wasn't ready to die just yet.

There was a back door to the office, and Esmeralda walked over and unlocked it.

"Take him out in the alley," she told Slade. "You can finish him there."

"You think it's a good idea just to shoot him down right here in town?"

"Do you think you can get him out of town? It didn't seem to work very well the last time you tried. I think the alley would be best."

"You're right," Slade said. He twitched the barrel of the shotgun just slightly. "You heard her, Fargo. The alley."

Fargo looked at the doorway. It opened into the night, and he couldn't see anything beyond it. He didn't really think there would be any help out there, anyway.

"You first," he said.

Slade gave a grunting laugh.

"A man ought not to joke when he's about to be killed," he said. "Now get out there."

Esmeralda moved well out of the way, behind the desk. Slade came out from behind the couch and stood waiting for Fargo to walk to the door.

Fargo stood where he was for a while, thinking about the possibilities. There didn't seem to be a whole lot of them. He started for the door.

"This time you won't be coming back, Fargo," Slade told him.

"We'll see," Fargo said.

Fargo walked right by a straight-backed wooden chair. Just as he was about to pass it, he hooked the toe of his boot around one leg of the chair and sent it flying toward Slade, who was now only a few feet away.

Before Slade knew what was happening, the chair hit him, knocking him off balance just enough for Fargo to pull the Colt while Slade was trying to bring the shotgun back in line. Slade didn't quite make it.

Fargo shot him twice. Both bullets hit him in the chest, in a space that could have been covered by a playing card. Slade looked down at himself, then looked back at Fargo. His eyes were already clouding over.

"You son of a bitch," Slade said, or tried to say. The last word was nothing but a mumble.

Slade sank to his knees. The shotgun barrel rested on the floor. Slade tried to bring it up with the last of his strength, but he couldn't quite make it. He did manage, however, to pull a trigger. The concentration of pellets blew a hole in the floor, and the force of the discharge knocked Slade over on his back. His right boot heel beat a brief tattoo on the floor, then stopped. The shotgun fell from his limp fingers and hit the floor, smoke curling up from it.

The shotgun blast was so loud in the small room that Fargo's ears were ringing. Esmeralda's mouth was moving, but he couldn't hear what she said. He figured she wasn't complimenting him on his shooting.

Esmeralda didn't waste any time grieving for Slade. Having said her piece, whatever it was, she jumped out the back door and disappeared into the alley. Fargo didn't believe in shooting anyone in the back, not even Esmeralda, so he let her go.

He bent down over Slade to see if he was still alive. If he was, he might be able to answer some questions for Fargo.

But Slade wasn't going to be answering any more questions for anybody, not unless it was Uncle Scratch.

The ringing in Fargo's ears was fading, and he could hear yelling and someone pounding on the door. It wouldn't be long before they broke it down. Fargo didn't want to be there when that happened. He went out into the alley, gun in hand, and closed the door behind him.

14

The alley was dark. Clouds had formed and bagged the moon and stars. Fargo could see dark outlines of the nearby buildings, but that was all. Esmeralda could have been standing no more than a few feet away and he wouldn't have known.

He didn't think she was there, though. He thought she was long gone. Exactly where she had gone was another question—and one Fargo couldn't answer.

He holstered his pistol and left the alley, mingling with the crowds on the street. He walked away from the Gypsy Queen and in the direction of the Iron Dog. He thought he might as well check in with Marian and make sure everything was all right. He could let her know that Slade wouldn't be bothering her again. And he could see if she'd found a bartender to replace Ray.

He took his time, making sure that no one from the Gypsy Queen was following him. He didn't want any trouble on the street. For that matter, he didn't want any trouble anywhere. He'd had enough of that for one night.

Fargo went in through the back door and passed through the kitchen. Wong wasn't there. He'd probably already gone home.

It seemed oddly quiet in the building, and at first Fargo didn't know why. Then he realized that the piano was silent.

That's one thing to be thankful for, he thought.

There wasn't much other noise, either. It was possible that the Gypsy Queen was drawing a bigger crowd, or maybe just a noisier one. Fargo went out into the main room.

There were quite a few people there, but no one was talking. People sat glumly, and nobody seemed to be having a very good time.

It didn't take Fargo long to figure out why. Sitting at a table right in the middle of the room was Deputy Marshal Sullivan. Sullivan had his pistol out, and it was pointed at Marian, who was sitting directly across the table from him. She looked like she'd like to bite Sullivan's ear off.

"Ah, Mr. Fargo," Sullivan said. "We've been expecting you."

So much for not wanting any more trouble, Fargo thought. He said, "I wasn't expecting you, though."

"Sure, and I'll wager you weren't," Sullivan said with a wide smile. "But I often turn up where I'm not expected." He had a private laugh at that as if it were a joke that only he knew. "Admit it, though. You're glad to see me now, aren't you, bucko."

"You talk too much," Fargo said.

Sullivan nodded and continued to smile.

"You have me there, Fargo. I admit it. The love of talk is the curse of the Irish. That and drinking, two things we dearly love. Except I gave up the bottle years ago. It makes a man's hand unsteady, and in my profession a steady hand is a great asset. But here I am, running on again when we have important business to conduct."

"What business?" Fargo asked.

He looked around the saloon to see if there was any help available. Glenn sat at his piano, looking at the floor. No help there. No help anywhere.

"It's like this, you see," Sullivan said. "I've recently been informed that someone killed a Mr. Slade in the Gypsy Queen. Shot him down like a dog. The poor man was unarmed and now he's been cut down in the very prime of his life. It's a shameful thing, Fargo, a shameful thing. Why just today I was here to arrest you for another murder, that of your fine friend Edwards, the barber, and here you've already killed again. You've been busy, boyo, very busy . . ."

"Did I mention that you talk too much?"

"You did, at that. You truly did. Very well, I'll stop. And you can come along to the jail with me."

"I didn't kill Edwards, and you know it. I killed Slade, though, and I won't deny it. I shot him in self-defense. He had a shotgun, and he was going to use it."

"That's your version of the affair, and you're entitled to it. I don't know that a judge will find it convincing in the face of the eye-witness testimony he'll be hearing."

Esmeralda, Fargo thought. Treacherous was the word, all right.

"Enough of that, though," Sullivan said. "It's time you were going."

"And if I don't?"

"Now there's the sad part, don't you see. If you don't, I'll be forced to put a bullet in Miss Marian here. Right between her pretty blue eyes."

"Cut her down in the prime of her life?"

"You're a clever man, Fargo, to turn my own words on me like that. But it's true. I'd do it. I'd do it with regret, but I'd do it, surely."

"I'll come then," Fargo said.

"No," Marian said. "He wouldn't shoot me, Fargo. But if you go, he'll kill you for certain."

Fargo figured that Sullivan would try, but there was always the chance he wouldn't succeed. So far, Fargo had proved pretty hard to kill.

"I'll go," Fargo said. "You don't need the pistol."

"Oh, but I'd love to think I didn't. But I believe I'll keep it where you can see it. You just go stand by the door, now, and when you're there I'll stop pointing this gun as Miss Marian."

Fargo walked over to the batwings. People shuffled out of his way as if he might be a smallpox carrier. They didn't meet his eyes.

When he got to the door, Fargo stopped, waiting to see what was next.

"You can come in now, boys," Sullivan called.

Two men entered the saloon. Barlow and Butler. They both had their guns out and ready. They appeared almost as happy as Sullivan to see him again.

"Your ass is ours now," Butler said, taking Fargo's Colt. "You won't be locking anybody in any jail cells for a long time after we get through with you."

"Never," Barlow said. He bent down and took the knife from Fargo's boot. "You'll never lock anybody up again. We're gonna have some fun with you, Fargo."

"You won't be having any fun, though," Butler said. "And that's a promise."

"Thanks for cheering me up," Fargo said. "It was shaping up to be a boring night."

"You have spirit, Fargo," Sullivan said, walking up to them. "I'll give you that. I like a man with spirit. It takes longer to break him."

"And you enjoy breaking people, don't you," Fargo said.

"One of my many weaknesses," Sullivan said. "I don't drink, mind you, so I feel I'm entitled to a few imperfections of character. But I'm talking too much again. Let's get on over to the jail."

Barlow and Butler stepped aside and Fargo went outside. The crowds in the street were not as quiet as the one in the saloon, but they were more subdued than usual. They knew that a dangerous man was being escorted to the jail. Otherwise, why would it take three men?

Sullivan liked being the center of attention, and he kept up a stream of chatter as they went along.

"Yes, indeed," he said to inquiring faces. "We have the man we've been looking for. A killer and a stagecoach robber, and God only knows what else he's done. A true desperado, one of the worst. But you can rest secure in your beds as long as Deputy Marshal Sullivan is on the job."

"Do you ever put a cork in it?" Fargo said.

Sullivan backhanded him across the mouth, smashing Fargo's lips and putting blood on his teeth. He staggered, and Butler caught him, then tossed him to Barlow, who shoved him down and kicked him in the ribs. Then he stomped his kidney. Fargo didn't move.

"You see how it is with these renegades," Sullivan said. "You have to use a rough hand to keep them in line."

Barlow and Butler grabbed Fargo under the arms and jerked him to his feet. They walked him along, supporting most of his weight themselves.

When they got to the jail, they threw Fargo roughly into the cell he'd occupied before. They stood outside the door until Sullivan got there. It took him a few minutes because he was regaling his adoring admirers with tales of his derring-do in the face of danger, as represented by miscreants like Fargo.

124

When Sullivan arrived, he was pulling on a pair of leather gloves. Barlow and Butler got out of his way and let him enter the cell with Fargo, who was lying on the cot.

"Well, me boy-o," Sullivan said. "It's you and I again, but this time the odds are in my favor." He nodded at Butler and Barlow. "Not that I need their help, mind you, but you've proved to be a tricky fella so the boys'll be keeping their guns on you while I give you a little lesson in humility."

Fargo looked up at Sullivan and said, "You're a yellow bastard, aren't you."

"Trying to make me angry, are you?" Sullivan said. "I don't blame you, old son. If I were angry, I might put you out of your misery in a hurry. I'm not angry, though, so I'm going to make you last a long time, Fargo. I believe I can promise you that. A long, long time. Now get up."

Fargo stayed where he was. Sullivan was going to make good on his promise, there was no doubt of that.

"I suppose you need a bit of help," Sullivan said. "Butler, help him up."

Butler started into the cell.

"Give Barlow your gun, bucko," Sullivan told him. "We wouldn't want Fargo to take it away from you, now would we."

Butler handed his pistol to Barlow and lifted Fargo to his feet. Fargo stood there, wavering slightly, and Butler went back outside the cell.

Sullivan hit Fargo with a short right to the stomach. As Fargo started to fold, Sullivan straightened him with a left to the jaw.

"That's more like it," Sullivan said.

Fargo knew it was going to be a long night.

Fargo saw the gray light of morning through the bars of the high cell window. His whole body ached. Even his hair ached. Sullivan was an expert, and he had gone quite a job. For the most part, he'd stuck to the parts of the body covered by clothing. Anyone looking at Fargo might not even know he'd been beaten.

Remove his clothing, however, and it would be a different

story. Fargo suspected that under his clothing, his entire body was just one big bruise.

At least his mind was still working, though no better than it had been before the beating. Nevertheless, he could remember one thing that Sullivan had said that added something new to the story. Sullivan had told one of the bystanders that Fargo was the stage robber. Fargo didn't have any idea how Sullivan was going to prove that, but he didn't doubt that the deputy marshal could do it. The evidence would be false, but that wouldn't matter to the judge, who was going to be shown that Fargo was a cold-blooded killer to boot, shooting down innocent unarmed men just for the fun of it.

Things were beginning to make a little more sense to Fargo now. Not complete sense, but a pattern was taking shape.

Fargo was going to be made the scapegoat for the stage robberies, which might explain why he hadn't been killed yet. They could have a trial, hang him, and show everyone how the police stopped the robberies. It might even work.

But why do it? As far as Fargo could tell, people in Virginia City weren't too worried about the robberies. They seemed to accept them as one of those things you have to put up with when you live in a booming mining town. Nobody had been killed yet, and according to most accounts, even the people who'd been robbed had been treated politely.

Fargo was still thinking it over when he heard a noise in the outside office. Someone yelled at someone else, there was some talking, and finally the door to the cell block opened.

Wong came cringing through the door. Butler stood behind him, cursing him for being a heathen.

"Yes, boss," Wong said. "You so right. Chinaman not good for nothing. But Missy Marian send soup for Mister Fargo, and Wong must bring it or Missy have him whipped. Please to open cell and let poor Chinaman give Mr. Fargo soup so Missy not hurt Wong."

"I don't give a damn if she stripes your back with a black-snake whip," Butler said. "You can give him the soup, but you ain't going in that cell."

"Oh, thank you boss," Wong said. "I give him soup between the bars. Chinaman can do that. You are too kind to poor Wong."

"Blow it out your ass," Butler said, and slammed the door.

Fargo sat up and said, "I wish you wouldn't do that. It hurts me to laugh. And don't you think you were laying the poor dumb Chinaman act on a little too thick? Even Butler might catch on after a while."

"Butler is like many of your countrymen," Wong said. "As long as he has someone to feel superior to, he does not suspect anything."

"I hope there's something he should have suspected," Fargo said. "I'm getting tired of this jail cell."

"There is the soup, for one thing," Wong said, holding up a large, thick bowl wrapped in a towel and covered by a lid. "It is Yee's special healing soup. I thought you might have need of it."

"You thought right. Sullivan worked me over until he was tired and had to go home to rest. He's probably still asleep."

"Then the soup will do you good. It has something added that will be even better. But first you must eat."

The bowl was too big to pass between the bars, so Wong held it while Fargo ate with a spoon that Wong provided. When he got near the bottom, the spoon chinked against something metallic. Fargo slipped the spoon beneath it and lifted it.

It was a gun, the one that gambler Williams had shot a man with in the Iron Dog. Fargo dried the pistol off and made sure there was no soup left in the barrel.

"Miss Marian knew I would be searched," Wong said. "And of course she was correct. But she didn't think anyone would search the soup. It is Yee's special soup. I told Missy Marian that it would do you good, but she thought the pistol would be more helpful."

"It's a good thing she was right about them not searching the soup," Fargo said. He had never even thought about where the gambler's pistol went. He was glad that Marian had picked it up. He inspected it. "It's even loaded."

"Miss Marian found a bullet somewhere. I think at the store near the saloon."

"Now all I have to do is get out of this cell," Fargo said.

"First finish the soup. Then we will see."

Fargo didn't argue. Whatever was in the soup, besides the pistol, was working its healing magic on him, and he was al-

127

ready feeling better. His body still ached, but not nearly as much as it had when Wong came in. The bowl was soon empty, and Fargo handed the spoon to Wong, who set both spoon and bowl on the floor. Then he started rummaging in his billowing pants.

"What are you looking for?" Fargo asked.

"Something else that Mr. Butler overlooked," Wong said, pulling a piece of wire out of his waistband.

While Fargo watched, Wong bent the end of the wire into an odd shape and stuck it in the lock on the cell door.

"Where did you learn to do that?" Fargo asked.

Wong smiled. "I learned many skills in China. I was something of a magician, though never very skilled. I was skilled enough, however, to open many doors. Yours are different, but they are not much of a challenge."

The lock clicked, and Wong pulled the door open.

"See what I mean?" he said.

Fargo didn't bother to answer. He came out of the cell and Wong pulled the door almost shut behind him.

"Now we will leave," Wong said. "You follow me."

Wong went to the door to the office and pounded on it.

"Please, boss," he called. "Poor Chinaman does not like jail. You let me out now."

Fargo heard Butler laugh on the other side of the door.

"You should stay in there a while. Do you a world of good."

"Please do not joke with poor Chinaman," Wong said. "Open door, please."

Fargo heard a key turn in the lock and stepped aside so that he was at least partially hidden behind Wong. Butler swung the door back, and Wong scuttled through.

"Thank you, boss," he said, drawing Butler's attention. "Chinaman leave this place now."

"Me too," Fargo said.

Butler's head snapped around so fast that it might have been on a spring, and Fargo stuck the barrel of the little one-shot gun right on the bridge of Butler's nose.

"Put your hands on your head," Fargo said, "I just have one shot, but it would sure scramble whatever's in that thick head of yours if you made me use it."

Butler put his hands on his head.

"Get his gun, Wong," Fargo said.

"Poor Chinaman do as told," Wong said, lifting Butler's pistol from its holster and handing it to Fargo, who took it and stepped back from Butler, covering him with his own gun.

Fargo slipped the gambler's gun into his pocket and looked around the office until he'd found his Colt.

"I think you said you didn't want to be locked in the cell again," Fargo said.

"That musta been Sullivan," Butler said. "I didn't say any such of a thing."

"Good. Because you're going back. Now."

Butler turned and walked through the doorway, keeping his hands on his head. When he was inside the cell and the door had been locked, Fargo said, "You can put your hands down now, Butler."

Butler let his hands fall and said, "We'll get you, Fargo. This time we'll kill you."

"You'd better," Fargo said. "Because if you don't, I'll be the one doing the killing."

15

"What will you do now, Fargo?" Marian asked.

They were sitting in the kitchen of the Iron Dog. Wong stood by the cookstove listening but not adding anything to the conversation.

"Keep out of Sullivan's sight," Fargo said, "until I can figure out this mess. It seems like he's always one step ahead of me. He knows when I'm not here, and he knows when I come back."

"I hope you don't think I'm telling him," Marian said.

"I might not know much, but I know better than that. Somebody must be telling him, though."

"It's not the girls. One of them was soft on Sullivan for a while, but that was before he beat her, the big bastard. She had bruises all over."

"So do I," Fargo said. "I could tell he was enjoying himself. I guess he enjoys it even more when he gets his hands on a woman."

"I haven't let him in the saloon since then," Marian said.

Fargo just looked at her.

"I mean I haven't let him in for anything other than his business. I can't keep him out when he represents the law."

"I guess not," Fargo said. "What do you know about the Silver King?"

"It's a big operation. They take a lot of silver out of the ground."

Something in Marian's tone made Fargo think she was telling a lot less than she knew.

"Everybody knows about the silver," he said. "I was hoping you might be able to tell me something about the operation, or about Sam King."

"What makes you think I know anything about Sam?"

"Just guessing," said Fargo, who really had no idea what was going on.

"I should've told you sooner," Marian said. "Sam is probably the reason Esmeralda and I don't get along."

"You mean it's not just the saloon?"

"Not entirely, but that's part of it. Sam and I used to be . . . good friends. Esmeralda wanted him, but she couldn't take him. I got tired of Sam, though, and he went to her. I don't think she ever got over being second choice."

That explained a lot of things, Fargo thought. It provided a connection between Esmeralda and King and through King there was a connection between Esmeralda and Slade. It also explained why Esmeralda was so eager to get Fargo onto that couch. She'd see it as another way of getting back at Marian. Fargo had been flattered to think it was his masculinity that made her so aggressive, but deep down he'd known better.

"That still doesn't tell us who's been spying on me," he said.

"It could be anybody," Marian said. "Even a customer."

Just then Glenn came into the kitchen.

"Fargo," he said. "What are you doing here? I thought you were in jail."

"I don't do too well in jails," Fargo said. "You looking for something?"

"I was hoping for a leftover biscuit," Glenn said, looking at Wong. "You got any?"

"All-ee biscuits gone," Wong said. "I fix-ee more for supper."

"All right," Glenn said. "You make good biscuits. I'm already looking forward to supper."

He went back out into the saloon, but Fargo didn't hear any off-key piano music.

"Do you really have to talk like that?" Fargo said. "Or is it that you just can't help yourself?"

"Poor Chinaman—"

"Stop it," Marian said. "You can talk good English here, Wong. Nobody thinks of you as a poor Chinaman."

Wong didn't look convinced to Fargo, who was wondering

why Glenn hadn't begun playing the piano yet. He said, "Wong, see if Glenn's in there. I don't want to show my face."

Wong took a peek out the door. He turned back and said, "He's not at the piano, and he's not at the bar."

"See how easy it is to talk right?" Fargo said.

Wong closed the door and walked back over by the stove.

"I'll give it a try," Wong said. "But only with you and Miss Marian."

"It's a start," Fargo said. "And now I think I'd better go."

"Where?" Marian asked.

"To find Glenn," Fargo said.

Fargo went out the back door and caught up with Glenn about thirty yards from the jail. He didn't waste time talking. He just grabbed the little piano player by the waist and picked him up like a sack of flour. Glenn was too surprised to squawk, and Fargo carried him into a nearby alley and set him on his feet.

"What the hell do you think you're doing?" Glenn said, adjusting his clothing.

"Nothing compared to what I'm going to do, you little weasel," Fargo said.

Glenn backed up a step, turning his head as if looking around for help. There wasn't any.

"I don't know what's got into you, Fargo," he said. "You're acting crazy."

"Nope, I'm acting smart for the first time. I don't know why it took me so long to figure out who was reporting to Sullivan on me. You were always there, always wanting to know where I was going. Every single time Sullivan turned up looking for me, you'd told him I'd be there. When Slade wanted to know when I was gone, you let him know."

"I don't know what you're talking about, Fargo. I wouldn't do anything like that to Marian. You're just wrong."

Glenn kept looking around in the alley, but there was still no one coming to his aid.

"I'm not wrong," Fargo said. "If I'm wrong, tell me why you were going to the jail just now."

"I wasn't going to the jail. I was just out for a walk. You

know how it is. Now and then a man needs to get outside for a little fresh air."

"You're mighty nervous for a fella who's just out for some fresh air," Fargo said.

Glenn turned to run. He managed only one step before Fargo got a hand on his scrawny neck and brought him to a halt.

"There's nothing down there at the end of the alley," Fargo said. He turned Glenn around. "We can talk right here."

Glenn didn't seem to want to talk. His left eyelid had started to twitch, and he was having trouble standing still. He acted like a man who was going to piss his pants if he didn't find a spot to relieve himself in the next few seconds.

"Well?" Fargo said.

Glenn said nothing. He opened his mouth, but no words came out. His lips trembled.

Fargo steadied Glenn with one hand and reached in a pocket with the other. He brought out the little pistol the dead gambler had dropped and stuck it squarely in the middle of Glenn's forehead. Doing that had made Butler very happy to do what Fargo told him, and Fargo figured it would work even better on Glenn.

"If I pull this trigger," Fargo said, "this little gun will hardly make a sound. Nobody in the street will hear it. Somebody might find you in the morning, but some dog will get to you first. I guess it won't matter to you what the dog does, whether he has a little bite to eat or just marks you."

It turned out that Glenn could talk, after all.

"For God's sake, Fargo!" he said. "You can't just shoot me and leave me here."

"Why not? I expect your friends Slade and Sullivan have done worse to people. You don't deserve any better."

"I didn't want to help them," Glenn said. "I had to do it. They would've killed me if I didn't."

"Then it seems to me I ought to kill you if you did."

"No, no." Glenn was practically whining now. "Maybe I can help you. Let me do something. Anything."

"There's nothing you can do for me you little sneak."

Fargo thumbed back the hammer of the pistol. Glenn's eyes got very wide. Then he sighed and closed them.

"Go ahead," he said. "Shoot me. You're right. I don't deserve any better."

"That's better," Fargo said. "Maybe I don't need to shoot you after all." The pistol went back into his pocket. "Just tell me what you know about Sullivan and Slade, and we'll be almost square."

"Almost?"

"You heard me. Now what do you know?"

Glenn swallowed hard. His adam's apple bobbed. He licked his lips.

"I'm waiting," Fargo said. "But I'm losing my patience."

"Well," Glenn said, "the trouble is, I don't know anything."

The small pistol appeared again. Fargo ground the end of the almost nonexistent barrel into Glenn's forehead.

"That's not what I want to hear," Fargo said.

"I swear to you," Glenn said. "On my mother's grave. I don't know anything."

"You have to know something. You couldn't do your spying if you didn't."

"That's just it. They didn't want me to know anything. After that night you whipped Slade, Sullivan sent word that he wanted to see me. You don't say *no* to a man like that, and I went. He told me that he wanted to know all about you."

"What did you tell him?"

"What could I tell him? Just that you came in with this bunch of men from Missouri and that you all seemed like good friends. And that you went to work for Marian after that. Sullivan said for me to keep an eye on you and that's what I did."

Fargo put the pistol away again.

"Did he pay you?" he asked.

"No. He didn't even offer to. He knew I'd do what he said. You don't know what kind of a man he is, Fargo. He would've killed me as easy as you step on a spider."

Fargo didn't think Glenn was much better than a spider, but he didn't see any profit in telling the piano player that. He said, "I know what Sullivan's like. Thanks to you."

"I didn't know he'd hurt you. I swear it."

Glenn was doing a lot of swearing. It was beginning to get on Fargo's nerves.

"No," he said, "you probably thought he'd just kill me."

134

"I didn't think that. I swear—"

Fargo put his hand over Glenn's mouth and stopped his voice.

"I don't think I ever heard so much lying from one man in such a short time," Fargo said. "Now you'll remember I told you we'd be almost square. Just nod if you do."

Fargo kept his hand over Glenn's mouth, but Glenn managed to nod.

"Good," Fargo said. "Now here's the rest of it. When I let go of you, you're going to walk out of this alley and down the street away from the jail. Understand?"

Glenn nodded again.

"All right. You'll be headed toward the saloon, but you're not going to stop there. You're going to keep right on going until you're out of town. I don't care where you go from there, but if I see you here again, I'm going to give you what Sullivan gave me. You got all that?"

Glenn nodded, but not with any enthusiasm. Fargo removed his hand and said, "Now get out of here."

Glenn walked to the entrance of the alley. He looked both ways, but he turned in the direction of the Iron Dog. Fargo went to the street and watched him until he was well past the Iron Dog.

I guess Marian will have to get herself a new piano player, Fargo thought.

Fargo didn't think it would be a good idea to go back to the saloon, even though there was now no one there to tell Sullivan where he was. There was somewhere else he could go, he thought, somewhere that would do him a lot more good than a night in a saloon. He started walking in the direction of Chinatown.

Yee came to the door in answer to Fargo's knock.

"I did not expect to see you again," she said.

Fargo liked women who didn't try to stake claims on him or get him to make promises to come back.

"I wanted to thank you for the soup," he said. "I could use some more of it, if you have any. Sullivan beat me up pretty bad."

"Come in," Yee said. "I think I have what you need."

135

That was a statement that could be taken two ways, and Fargo hoped she meant both of them. When she led him to the bedroom they'd used before, he was pretty sure she did.

"You wait here," she said. "I will bring the soup."

She lit the lamp and left the room, closing the door behind her. Fargo waited until she returned with a steaming hot bowl of soup.

"I think you are able to feed yourself this time," she said, putting the soup on the table with the lamp.

"I might look good with my clothes on," Fargo said, "but under them I'm just one big ugly bruise."

"You might be bruised, but I suspect that you are not ugly."

"There's a way to find out."

"We will see about that. First, you eat your soup."

"Yes, ma'am," Fargo said, and he did.

The soup was so hot that Fargo had to blow on each spoonful before eating it. He didn't remember that it had been that hot before, but he remembered the sweet and spicy taste. And he remembered how it had made him feel. The bowl that Wong had brought to the jail had helped him immensely. This bowl was going a long way to making him as good as new.

When he finished, he put the spoon on the table and said, "That was good. I really appreciate your help. You and your brother have been very good to me."

"You have been good to us. We are simply returning the favor. Would you like for me to look at those bruises? I have some salve that might help them."

Fargo didn't wait for a further invitation. He started shucking off his clothes. When he was naked, Yee looked at him and said, "As usual, not all parts of you were affected by what happened."

Fargo looked down to see that his pole was standing at stiff attention.

"I guess it's being in the same room with you," he said. "Just seems to do something to me."

"I think you must have said that to many women."

Fargo thought about it. Truth to tell, there had been a lot of them, and he had enjoyed them all.

"Maybe not as many as you think," he said.

Yee opened a drawer in the table where the soup was. She

took out a small jar, opened it, and dipped her fingers inside. She brought out a white, shiny substance and rubbed her hands together to get it on both of them.

"I will put this on your bruises," she said.

She ran a slick hand over his chest, and Fargo felt his erection twitch upward.

"How does that feel?" she asked.

"Good," Fargo said. "Real good."

"I think you are feeling it somewhere that I didn't intend," Yee said.

She spread the salve over his bruises, then got more from the jar. She touched a scar where a grizzly had left its mark.

"Some woman must not have liked you," she said.

"That was a bear," Fargo said with a laugh. "And I can promise you that we weren't making love."

Yee let her fingers trail down Fargo's chest to his stomach, and then even lower. Her fingernails were long and sharp, and she touched the tender skin on the end of his penis with them.

"You trust me a great deal," she said, "to let me do this."

Her fingernails dug in a little deeper.

"I know you wouldn't hurt me," Fargo said, looking into her deep black eyes.

"No, I would never do that," Yee said.

She began to massage him with her warm, slick hand, rubbing him easily and slowly, letting her attention linger at the sensitive tip, which she squeezed until it slipped out of her hand. When it did, she began her massage again. Fargo felt a tingling sensation that ran all the way down to his toes.

"Now I will clean you," Yee said.

She knelt down and took him in her hot, sweet mouth.

Fargo's calf muscles clenched as she began to move her mouth up and down his shaft, teasing it with her tongue at the same time. He didn't know how she was doing it, and he didn't care, as long as she didn't stop.

But after a while, he wanted her to stop because if she didn't, she was going to drain him before he got to pleasure her. He reached down to her head, which was covered with a black curtain of hair, and lifted gently.

"It's your turn now," he said.

Yee didn't hesitate. She threw off her clothes and got onto

the bed, spreading her legs for him. He started to kiss her at the base of her navel and worked his way down.

Her lean body quivered with anticipation, and soon his tongue was easing itself into the narrow opening between her thighs. He played around the edges at first and then slipped it between the lips and found the tense little cartilage that was the center of her being at that moment. He flicked it once, and she gasped. He flicked it again, and her body shook.

When the tremors had stopped, she pulled her knees back until they were almost touching her ears.

"Go inside," she said. "I want to feel you there."

Fargo started to ease himself into her, but she put her arms around him and pulled him to her hard, so that he went in fast and completely. She locked her ankles behind his back and held him there, immobile.

"I just want to enjoy the way it feels inside me," she said breathily.

They stayed like that for a while. Fargo didn't know how long. But he did know that after a few seconds, the muscles inside her started to perform tricks that he would have said were impossible, squeezing him from tip to root in a series of rippling movements. Yee began to move her hips, rocking him gently, prompting him to rock with her. Soon he was thrusting, withdrawing only a short distance at first and them pulling out farther with each stroke until only the tip remained inside her. Then he plunged all the way in, stopped, and pulled back out again.

"Now," she said. "I must have it now."

With that, she used her legs to drive Fargo all the way in and hold him there as she quivered from head to toe and dug her sharp nails into his back.

Fargo was unable to hold back any longer, and he poured himself into her, shooting so strongly that the muscles in his neck contracted.

"*Eeeeeeeeeee*," Yee said, so low that if she hadn't had her mouth right by Fargo's ear he might not have heard her. "*Ahh-hhhhhhhhh.*"

When he was finally emptied, Fargo didn't withdraw, and soon he felt himself growing hard again.

Yee plainly enjoyed the sensation of his size increasing inside her. She wiggled her hips to encourage him, and when he was ready she bucked him like a young bronc. She was so enthusiastic that he was afraid they might fall off the bed, but he matched her fervor with an ardor of his own. Soon she opened her mouth to cry out, but before she did, she bit down on her wrist to stop herself.

As they rested on the bed afterward, Yee said, "You are much of a man, Fargo. I am glad to have met you."

"And I'm mighty glad you met me," Fargo said. "I never knew anybody quite like you."

"Not even among the many women you have loved? Not even Esmeralda or Marian?"

"You know about them?"

"Everyone knows about Marian. But not about the other one, who calls herself a gypsy queen."

"You seem to know a lot, though."

"We Chinese know many things, as Wong has no doubt told you."

"But you don't know enough to help me," Fargo said. "I wish you did."

"Perhaps if you explained your problem, I could help more than you think."

Fargo looked at her in the lamplight. Her face was partly in shadow, but she was even more beautiful than he had thought when he first saw her. He kissed the nipples of her small but perfect breasts, and she held his head to her.

"That is very nice," she said, "but it is not solving your problem."

"I can think of one problem it would solve."

"Not even you can have that problem again so soon. Tell me about your other difficulty."

Fargo considered it and then thought he might as well. Wong knew most of it, so there was no harm in telling Yee. It took him a while, but he got it told.

"If the men who were killed had nothing in common where they came from," she said, "then they must have been killed because of something that happened here."

"I got that far with it," Fargo said. "But nothing's happened here."

"Many things happen in Virginia City."

"Yeah, that's true, but what do they have to do with me and those men from Missouri? Nothing, as far as I can tell."

Fargo let his fingers play over the nipples of Yee's breasts. The nipples stiffened, and Fargo's fingers drifted lower.

Yee took hold of his wrist and moved his hand to her side.

"You are making it difficult for me to concentrate."

"You could concentrate on something different," Fargo said.

"Later, perhaps. Now we are thinking about your problem. Why would they want to blame you for the stagecoach robberies?"

"To make people think they were getting something done," Fargo said.

"Or to take the blame away from the real robbers. There have been rumors about that for some time now."

"I haven't heard 'em," Fargo said.

"The rumors might not have been spread in your part of the town. But here, we have heard them. They concern someone you know all too well, someone who is not well thought of by my people."

"Who would that be?"

"The deputy marshal. Sullivan."

"Your people are not the only ones who don't like him."

"But we have more reason. He is brutal to you, perhaps, but he is more brutal to any Chinese that he can catch doing wrong. Or any Chinese that he can blame for doing wrong, whether there is guilt or not."

"He's a mean son of a bitch," Fargo said. "No doubt about it."

"He is more than mean. People here say he is the leader of the stage robbers."

For some reason the rumor didn't surprise Fargo. It was always a disappointment to hear that a lawman might actually be a lawbreaker, but it wouldn't be the first time Fargo had encountered such a thing. And Sullivan's brutality showed that the man had a tendency to cross the line between enforcing the law and satisfying his own perversions.

Fargo thought back over his encounters with Sullivan and remembered the deputy marshal having said something about turning up in places people didn't expect. Maybe he'd been making a little joke about his illegal activities.

"He had to have some help," Fargo said.

"The man called Slade. He was the one."

"He won't be helping any more," Fargo said.

"So Wong has told me. You are a very busy man, Fargo."

"I like to keep my hand in." Fargo slid his fingers between Yee's legs and fondled her. "If you know what I mean."

"Was there ever any doubt? But that is not exactly what we were discussing."

Fargo got his mind back on important matters, not that his interest in Yee wasn't important.

"All right," he said. "Sullivan and Slade were in on the robberies together. And they're somehow tied to the Silver King. That still doesn't tell us who killed Nelson, Edwards, and Taylor."

"Does there have to be any connection between their deaths and the Silver King? Maybe your thinking is leading you away from the right answer."

"Maybe so. But it seems to me there's something going on, and it even seems to me I ought to know what it is. I just can't quite put my finger on it."

"In that case," Yee said, "I can think of something for you to put your finger on."

"What would that be?" Fargo asked. "This?"

"Ah. Yes. That would be it."

"What if I did this?"

"Oh. Oh. Please. Do it. Do it!"

Fargo did.

16

It was late when Fargo left, but he was feeling much better than when he'd arrived. He didn't know whether it was the soup or the salve or the romp with Yee. It could have been a combination of all three things, but whatever it was, he hardly felt the effects of Sullivan's attentions.

He was thinking more clearly, too, or he thought he was. But he couldn't be sure if he was on the right track until he talked to someone who knew more about silver mining than he did.

It so happened that he knew a couple of men who knew something about silver mining, though he wasn't sure just how much. He headed in the direction of Utley and Carter's claim. He had only a vague idea of where the Missouri Beauty was but he thought he could find it.

It turned out to be a little more difficult than he'd thought, especially in the dark, because there were so many holes in the ground, so many little mining shacks, so many badly lettered signs proclaiming ownership.

He eventually found the one that announced the Missouri Beauty. True to form, there was nothing beautiful about it that Fargo could see. It was just a hole in the mountain with a few bushes around. The shack where Utley and Carter were staying was no better. In fact, it might have been worse. The walls were full of cracks and the roof didn't look as if it would keep the rain out. Fargo figured that when winter came, it would be just as cold inside the place as it was on the outside. The walls wouldn't do much to stop the wind or to keep the snow from piling up on the floor.

There was no light in the shack, but Fargo hadn't really expected one. It was too late, and Utley and Carter, tired from

142

their day's work in their mine, had probably gone to sleep early. Fargo didn't feel guilty about waking them, however. It was for their benefit as much as his. Maybe more for their's.

He walked up to the door and banged on it with his open palm. It rattled loosely in its ill-fitting frame.

"What the hell's all the noise about?" someone called from inside.

Fargo recognized Utley's voice. He said, "It's Fargo. Let me in. We need to have a talk."

Fargo heard some shuffling around inside and some muttering between Utley and Carter. Someone lit a lantern, and the light shone through the cracks in the boards. Then Utley spoke to Fargo from the other side of the door.

"How do we know it's Fargo and not some sorry-assed claim jumper?"

"Because I'm the one that brought you here from Missouri and you should know my voice by now."

"I guess it's Fargo, all right," came Carter's voice. "Let him in."

A board was moved on the inside and Utley slipped the latch. The door opened and Fargo saw Utley standing there, a pistol in his hand and the light behind him. The pistol was pointed right at Fargo's belt buckle.

"I knew you'd be glad to see me," Fargo said.

"It ain't that we don't like you," Carter said from the other side of the room where he stood holding a pistol of his own. "It's just that we're a little bit jumpy these days. You can't blame us for that, now, can you."

Fargo admitted that he couldn't blame them. Utley and Carter were ordinary men who now found themselves in unusual circumstances. Someone had killed the others who'd recently come from Missouri, and that same someone might go after them next. Fargo was sure that this was a first for both of them.

"So, are you going to invite me in, or should I just stand here so you can admire me?" he asked.

Utley backed out of the way, but he didn't lower his pistol. Fargo stepped inside and looked around. The view wasn't any more impressive than it had been from the outside. There was a hard-packed dirt floor, an old table that might have been saved from somebody's junk pile, and one rickety chair. There were no beds, just a couple of pallets on the floor.

"Glad to see you trust me," Fargo said to Utley.

"Trust ain't got nothing to do with it. Me and Carter just want to stay alive long enough to see this little mine of ours pay off."

"Any day now," Carter said. He lowered his pistol. "Any day."

Both men had been sleeping in their work clothes. There was a smell of sweat and dust in the shack. Utley, still holding his pistol, asked what Fargo was doing there in the middle of the night.

"Trying to get a few things straight in my mind," he said.

"What things?" Utley asked.

"Things about silver mining," Fargo said. "I figured you two would be the ones to know."

"This have anything to do with Taylor and the others?" Carter wanted to know.

"It might. Might not. That's what I'm hoping you can help me with."

Utley appeared to decide that Fargo wasn't there to rob or kill them. He stuck his pistol in his waistband and said, "I'd offer you a seat, but as you can see, we ain't got but the one. And it's in mighty sad shape. Might collapse under you if you was to sit in it."

"I'll stand," Fargo said. "I don't mind."

"Sorry not to be more hospitable. Now what did you want to know about mining?"

"I want to know what you're looking for."

Carter and Utley looked at each other and laughed.

"Silver," Carter said when he'd stopped. "We're looking for silver, just like every other poor son of a bitch in this place."

Fargo had wondered what was so funny. Now he knew. They'd misunderstood his question.

"I know you're looking for silver," he said. "That's not what I meant."

"What the hell did you mean, then?" Utley said.

"I mean what are you looking for that lets you know the silver is around. It doesn't come out of the ground in bars."

144

"Well, why didn't you say so? If you put it that way, what we're looking for is the right kind of dirt."

Fargo knew that, too. He'd finally figured out something that he'd been bothered by on his second visit to the Silver King.

"Tell me about the right kind of dirt," he said.

"Well," Carter said, "first of all, it's not exactly dirt. And if you didn't know exactly what you were looking for, you'd miss it. The first miners that came up here nearly missed it themselves, and when they found it, they didn't know what to do with it."

"That's the damn' truth," Utley said. "Most of 'em were from California, and they were looking for gold. They thought it would be like it is in California, more or less lying on top of the ground or under the water of some little creek."

"But it's not," Fargo said.

"Hell, no, it's not." Utley shook his head. "Here, you gotta dig for it. You know that. Some of these mines go away underground already, and they'll go a lot deeper before they're played out."

"That's the way it is with us," Carter said. "We just gotta go deeper, and then we're gonna hit it."

He sounded more like he was trying to convince himself than Fargo.

"Let's get back to the dirt," Fargo said.

"Yeah," Utley said. "Well, like I said, most of the early miners here were looking for gold, and by God they found that, too. But they didn't know much about mining it, so some of them sold their claims for next to nothing, like the man they called Old Virginny. They named the town for him, but he didn't make much from his claim."

"The dirt," Fargo said.

"Sure. Sure. Since they were looking for gold, they almost missed the silver because it was in a funny blue-colored sand. They knew there wasn't any gold in sand like that, so they just thought it was a worthless aggravation. It wasn't till later that they found out how much money it was going to be worth to them."

"So that's what you're looking for," Fargo said. "Blue sand."

"That's right," Carter said. "And we'll find it, too. We explored around pretty good, and I'll bet you we're standing right on top of a vein of that sand that's going to make me and Utley two of the richest men in Nevada Territory."

Maybe he believed that if he kept saying it often enough it would happen, Fargo thought. He said, "I think you've told me what I wanted to know. Now I have a favor to ask."

Utley was immediately suspicious. He said, "You wanting to buy into our claim?"

"Nothing like that," Fargo said. "I was just wondering if you could put me up for the night."

Carter looked at the pallets and then back at Fargo.

"You can see we don't exactly have the nicest accommodations. We might have an extra blanket to spread somewhere if that's good enough for you."

"We slept in some worse places than this when we came out here from Missouri," he said. "A blanket on the floor would do me just fine."

"I'll look for the blanket, then," Utley said.

The next morning Fargo was a little sore from the effects of the bruises combined with sleeping on the floor, but he wasn't nearly as sore as he would have been had he not been ministered to by Yee.

He had finally figured it all out, or at least he thought he had. On his visit to the stamp mill at the Silver King, he'd noticed that everything was covered with black dust. That might not have been suspicious if the mine had been producing gold, but it wasn't. It was producing silver.

Or maybe it wasn't. Fargo hadn't seen any sign of blue sand. He told himself that he might have figured things out sooner if he hadn't been hit on the head while he was looking things over. A knock like that was enough to addle anybody.

The way Fargo had worked it out, there wasn't any silver in the Silver King and never had been. Oh, there might have been a little something at first, enough to keep Sam King encouraged for a while, but it must have played out quickly, leaving King with just another of the many worthless claims on Davidson Mountain.

But he'd figured out a way to make it pay off. All he had to do was keep operating his mine and get his silver somewhere else. Somewhere like the stagecoach that often carried silver bars out of town. Sullivan and Slade didn't have to take the silver to California. They just took it to King's mine. Then, a few weeks later, King could send the silver off himself, on the same stage line. Fargo would have been willing to bet a year's earnings that the stage had never been robbed while King's silver was on it.

It was a clever scheme. As long as nobody looked at King's operation too closely, he could get away with it. No wonder he was sensitive about people coming around the mine. He didn't want anybody to see exactly what was going on, which was pretty much nothing. He was breaking rock and sifting it, but he wasn't getting any silver out of it.

It hadn't taken Taylor long to figure it out, and Taylor's problem was that he had a conscience. He'd come to Nevada Territory because of it. King could probably buy off all his other men, but Taylor must have been a different story. So of course he had to be gotten out of the way.

But there was another problem. Who might Taylor have told about King's fake mine? Taylor had come to the territory with several friends, one of whom was a preacher. What if Taylor had told him about the mine? And then there was Edwards, the barber. What if Taylor had let something slip when he was getting a haircut? Better get the preacher and the barber out of the way, too, just to be sure everything was covered.

Then there was Fargo. He'd led the men to Virginia City. What if Taylor had trusted him with the information about King? Better see to it that he didn't tell anyone. Or, even better, blame the stage robberies on him and take care of him that way. Lay off the robberies for a while to let everyone believe that Fargo was guilty, then start robbing again and put out the word that it was a different gang doing the jobs. It would cut the income for a while, but then it would be back to business as usual. If, that is, Fargo didn't do something about it.

So now there was only one question left: What was Fargo going to do?

He didn't know. He was only one man, and King had Sullivan and no telling how many other men at the mine. There might be some who didn't know what was going on, but if there were, they'd be in a minority. Going up against them would be like going up against a small army. What Fargo needed was an army of his own.

Maybe he could find one.

"I am not sure," Wong said. "Some of the men I know would be willing to do it, but we are not looked upon with favor here. If we do not prevail, we will all be beaten or hanged. Possibly both."

"So will I," Fargo pointed out.

"For some reason that does not comfort me," Wong told him.

"I can see why. But what if we win? You'll all be heroes. You'll have found out who's responsible for the stage robberies, and you'll put a killer or two behind bars."

"In this case, the killer is the one who usually puts people behind bars. I am not sure I believe people will think him guilty."

"Plenty of people must know what kind of man Sullivan is. They won't be surprised to find out he's behind those robberies."

"But what of Mr. King? He is a respected man. No one will believe he could be involved in illegal enterprises."

"That'll be the easy part," Fargo said. "We'll just show them the setup at the mining operation. When they see there's no silver there, they'll be convinced."

Fargo and Wong were sitting in the kitchen of the Iron Dog, and while they were talking, Marian came in.

"What's this about Sam King?" she asked.

Fargo explained as quickly as he could.

"I can believe it," Marian said. "That mine of his was going nowhere, and everyone thought he'd be gone soon enough. But not long after he took up with Esmeralda, he struck it rich. Or said he did. Now you're telling me he didn't."

"He struck it rich, all right," Fargo said. "He just figured out a way to do it without actually mining any silver."

A thoughtful look crossed Marian's face. She said, "I wonder if Esmeralda knows."

"She might," Fargo said. "I guess it depends on how much she knows about mining—or how much King trusted her."

"My experience with him was that he didn't trust anybody very much."

"Then maybe she doesn't know. Anyway, she won't be involved in this."

"In what?" Marian asked, and Fargo had to explain what he'd been proposing to Wong.

"You want to take a bunch of Chinamen out there to the Silver King and take it over? You'd never be able to do that, even without Sullivan against you."

"We weren't planning to let Sullivan in in our plans," Fargo said. "Seen Glenn lately?"

"No. I'm getting worried about him. It's not like him to go off without telling me."

"He didn't leave on his own," Fargo said, and told her about the piano player.

"Why the dirty little skunk. I gave him a job when nobody else in town would."

"You'll have to find yourself another piano player," Fargo said. "I don't think he'll be coming back. And with him gone, I don't think anybody will tell Sullivan our plans."

"You can't be sure about Sullivan. He's a devious man."

"I know. We'll just have to hope he doesn't show up at the wrong time. Anyway, Wong still hasn't said he'd help."

"I have been thinking," Wong said. "I owe you the favor of helping you, and I believe my friends would be willing to help. So I will ask."

"I don't want you doing this because you think you owe me something," Fargo said. "If you do it, just do it because we're friends."

Wong smiled. "It is too bad that there are not more men in Virginia City like you, Fargo. It would be a better place."

"You forgot to call me *mister*."

"That is because we are friends, are we not?"

"Yeah," Fargo said. "We are."

17

Fargo walked up to the open door of the mining shack that Sam King used for an office. King must have seen him coming because he stepped outside and stood in front of the building.

"You got a lot of nerve coming back here, Fargo. I'll have to give you that. I thought you'd found out that snooping around here wasn't a good idea. You might wind up in a worse spot than you did last time."

"I don't think so," Fargo said. "This time I have some help."

King looked beyond Fargo. Then he looked to the left and to the right.

"I don't see anybody," he said. "Come out here, Howard."

A man came out the door and stood beside King. He was big and mean-looking like nearly everybody who worked for the mine owner.

"This here is the fella who killed Rascoe," King said. "You remember I told you about him."

"Yeah," Howard said. "I remember."

"And you remember what I told you to do if he ever set foot on my property again?"

"You said to beat the shit out of him and then kill him."

"Those might not have been my exact words, but that's close enough. What are you waiting for?"

"Not a damn thing," Howard said, starting for Fargo.

Fargo pulled out his Colt and shot Howard in the right knee. The big man howled and went down.

"You should have told him to kill me and then beat me up," Fargo said. "Did you think I was going to wait for him to do it?"

King looked at Howard, who was writhing in pain on the ground.

"I didn't think you'd do something that stupid," King said. "And then Howard's not exactly the smartest man on the mountain. Doesn't matter, though. I got plenty of other men."

King put his right thumb and forefinger at the corners of his lips and gave out a piercing whistle that could be heard even over the noise of the stamp mill. Men came out and stood waiting for King to tell them what to do.

"See how many of 'em there are?" King said. "You shouldn't have come here, Fargo."

"You could be right," Fargo said. "On the other hand, you could be wrong. I could just shoot you and have done with it."

"I'm unarmed, and there are too many witnesses. Besides, I don't think you'd do a thing like that. Which is why I win and you lose."

"You haven't won anything yet," Fargo said.

He took off his hat and waved it in the air. Wong and his friends appeared from behind rocks, from behind bushes, and even from behind the stamp mill. Some of them were armed with pistols. Others had only knives. A few had small axes. There were quite a few of them. More than Fargo had hoped for, in fact. They actually had King and his men outnumbered.

King looked the situation over and said, "Seems like I keep underestimating you, Fargo. I should have known you'd have somebody at your back."

Howard said something, or tried to. Fargo couldn't quite make it out, but it sounded like he was saying that maybe King wasn't as smart as he thought he was.

"Oh, shut up, Howard," King said. "Look, Fargo, we can work something out here."

"You mean you'll admit that you had Taylor, Nelson, and Edwards killed? And that you've been taking your silver off the stage instead of mining it?"

"Why should I admit that? It's not true."

"The hell it's not," Fargo said.

"Even if it was true, you could never prove it."

"I think I can. If you'll come back to town with me, we'll let the law decide."

King smiled like a man who had the law in his pocket.

151

"I'm not talking about Sullivan," Fargo said. "We'll talk to some of the other lawmen. Get a real judge. The way it's supposed to be done."

"You know something, Fargo?" King said.

"No. What?"

"You can go to hell," King said.

He turned and jumped back inside the shack. As if at some unseen signal, the men from the stamp mill pulled their guns and opened fire. Wong and his men charged out of their positions and attacked.

Fargo would have liked to stay around and watch the fun. He had a feeling the miners were going to be surprised by what happened to them, but the one he was really after was King.

The shack had a back door, and it was wide open. King had gone out and headed for the mine. Fargo could see that there was someone with him.

It was Esmeralda. She wasn't dressed as she'd been at the Gypsy Queen, but Fargo recognized her even in riding pants and a shirt. She must have been talking something over with King. Maybe they were plotting another attack on the Iron Dog.

Before they got to the mine entrance, Esmeralda turned aside and ran down a trail that wound through the bushes. Fargo didn't know where she was going, but he knew he'd better stick with King. If he let the mine owner get too far ahead, he'd be impossible to find in the depths of the mine. He'd know where to go, where all the tunnels led, which ones were dangerous and which ones weren't. He'd know how to get back out after he'd wound around in the honeycombed mountainside. Fargo didn't plan to let him get away, which meant he had to stick with him.

When King disappeared inside the mine entrance, Fargo was only a few yards behind.

Even with lanterns to light the way it was dark inside the mine. Fargo saw a place where a lantern was missing. He could see the light bobbing along ahead of him, dangling from King's hand. Fargo figured that King planned to go down a few tunnels where there wouldn't be any lanterns, so Fargo grabbed a light for himself and followed.

King was moving fast, with the sure confidence of a man who knew his way around under the earth. Fargo was hesitant, not knowing when he might step on a rock or into a crack. He had to be careful. So King gained a little ground on him.

They went steadily downward, and Fargo could hear men working below. He didn't think there would be many men there, and they wouldn't be working very hard, just doing enough to keep up appearances. After all, they weren't really working a vein. The tunnels that King fled through had been dug when there was hope he'd find something. The new tunnels no doubt grew very slowly if at all.

King abruptly disappeared. He'd made a sharp turn into a branch tunnel. Fargo approached it cautiously. When he reached the entrance, he eased his head around for a look. He couldn't see King's light, which could mean that King had taken another turn.

Or it could mean that King was lurking a few yards ahead, just waiting for Fargo to come to him.

Fargo wondered if King would dare to fire a pistol. The main tunnel was braced up pretty well, but he didn't think all the tunnels would be fitted out with square set timbering.

Fargo put out his own lantern and entered the tunnel as quietly as he could. He walked a few steps and waited for his eyes to become accustomed to the dark.

They didn't. With only the dimmest of lights behind him in the main tunnel, it was far too dark inside this one for him to see anything at all. It was as dark as the inside of a cow's belly. Fargo knew that after he took a few more steps, he wouldn't be able to see his hand in front of his face, not even if he held it within inches of his nose.

Why had King run into a place like that? There could be only one reason, Fargo thought. King must know this particular tunnel well enough to find his way around in complete darkness. That didn't bode too well for someone like Fargo, and this time there weren't any tracks for him to follow back.

Fargo stood still, listening, hoping that King would give his position away. The only thing Fargo could hear was the faint sound of men working in some other tunnel, and the sound of shooting and yelling from outside.

I should just get the hell out of here and leave him, Fargo thought. Wong probably needed help, and Fargo knew that King would have to come out of the mine sooner or later. But he might not have to come out the main entrance. What if King knew of another way out? It was entirely possible that some tunnel in the mine had another exit. If King could get out that way, he'd be over the mountains and lost in California. Fargo couldn't let him escape that easily. He owed him a beating or two. Keeping that thought in mind, Fargo went down the tunnel into the darkness.

Fargo walked close to the tunnel wall, keeping a hand on it, moving as quietly as a cat on velvet. He put his feet down carefully so as not to turn an ankle on a loose rock and have the resulting noise send a signal to King that would give away his location. At the same time he listened, hoping that King would betray his own position.

After he'd gone about twenty-five yards, he came to a place where the tunnel branched. There was a gaping opening on his right, and when he crossed it, he could tell that the tunnel he was in ran on straight ahead. He stopped to think things over. He had no idea which way King had gone, and the total darkness was beginning to play tricks with his sense of direction. He was no longer even sure he could find his way out if he stayed right by the wall and went back the way he'd come. He wasn't sure which way that was. He was afraid that if he stayed in the total darkness much longer, he was going to lose all sense of direction and perspective.

It was then that he heard something from the branch tunnel. He looked down it and thought he saw a brief flash of light as someone turned a corner.

It had to be King. He was in the same situation as Fargo, and the darkness was affecting him as well. Maybe knowing where he was headed wasn't such a great comfort. So he'd lit his lantern, making the noise that Fargo had heard.

Fargo decided that it wouldn't hurt to light his own lantern now that King was out of sight. The flash of the lucifer was almost blinding, and the light emitted by the lantern when Fargo got it lit was more comforting than a bowl of Yee's soup. Fargo had never known that a dim light could make a person feel so secure. Its yellow glow diminished the shadows and made the walls plain. Fargo grinned and started after King.

Now that he could see, he noticed that the tunnel was sloping downward pretty sharply. They must have been serious about finding silver at first, and it had probably been a big disappointment to King when there was no payoff. Of course a lot of other men had been disappointed, and they hadn't turned to robbery to make a profit.

As the tunnel continued to dip, Fargo saw that occasionally there was an abandoned pickax or hammer lying near the wall. He wondered if King had picked one up for some close-quarters work. Fargo bent down and took one. The handle was solid, if dirty, and the pick was beginning to show a little rust.

It was warmer now, and Fargo wondered how far down he'd gone. Not that it mattered. If he died down here, a foot from the entrance was no better than a mile. He kept on walking. Even with the light, however, it wasn't long before the walls seemed to be closing in on him and the roof seemed to be getting lower and lower.

At first Fargo told himself it was all his imagination and that he shouldn't worry about it, but then he realized that he wasn't imagining things at all. The tunnel really was narrowing, and the ceiling was indeed lower. He had to crouch in order to move forward.

Again he was glad he had the light. If he hadn't, he might not have trusted his instincts. No telling what might have happened then.

At the turning of the tunnel, however, Fargo had to extinguish the lantern. He didn't want to give King any sight of him. The darkness and silence closed around him. It seemed almost to have a solidity and weight heavier than the sod of the grave, the narrow walls could soon become his coffin if he wasn't careful.

Fargo shook off his morbid thoughts and told himself that there was one good thing. After the turn, the tunnel appeared to widen again, and the ceiling was high enough so that he could almost stand. The tunnel seemed to take a slightly upward slope, too, which might mean that he was heading back out of it. If that were true, it would be welcome news.

And besides that, Fargo thought he saw an indistinct glimmer of light when he took a quick glance around the turn. If King hadn't damped his lantern, he was either getting jittery in the dark, or he thought he'd managed to lose Fargo somewhere in the mine.

Well, Fargo wasn't lost, and he wasn't far behind. He made sure his own lantern was out and turned the corner.

Once again he was in total darkness. Whatever glimpse of light he might have seen had disappeared completely.

Fargo stopped where he was. Could the light have been a trick? Was King just making sure that Fargo could follow him? It was possible. And if that was the case, what did King have in mind.

Only one way to find out, Fargo told himself, and felt his way along the wall, touching it with one hand and holding the pick and the wire handle of the lantern tight in the other. If there was going to be a fight, the pick would come in mighty handy since Fargo didn't plan to shoot a pistol down there unless he was forced to. He didn't like to think of the walls falling in and trapping him in the dark. Hell, he didn't like to think about being trapped even with the lantern on.

And speaking of hell, it was getting hotter in the tunnel. At least Fargo hoped it was. He wiped sweat from his forehead. He wouldn't like to think he was sweating because he was nervous. He touched the wall again. It was definitely warmer than it had been before. Rock should be cold to the touch, not warm. Maybe hell was right on the other side.

Fargo was shaken out of his brooding when he heard a faint *clink* up ahead. He stopped where he was to listen. The sound didn't come again, but Fargo was sure he'd heard it, and it had been the sound of metal on stone. There was only one person who could have made that sound. King. And he was somewhere only a few yards away in the darkness.

Fargo prided himself on being able to move silently, but he knew that no one could completely avoid making some kind of sound every now and then, no matter how careful he might be.

156

So maybe King had heard him coming and was waiting up ahead to ambush him.

Or maybe King was doing nothing of the kind. He could have been resting, with not a thought of Fargo in his head.

Fargo guessed it didn't matter. Either way, King was there, and Fargo knew it. Now he had to do something about it.

First, he put down the lantern so he could hold the pick with both hands if he had to. He set the lantern on the floor of the tunnel moving so slowly that he might have been mired in molasses. When it touched stone, there was not so much as a click. Fargo raised himself up, gripped the pick hard in one hand, and felt his way with the other. He breathed as shallowly as possible so that the air made no sound either coming in or going out. After every step, he stopped to listen for King.

He judged that he'd gone about ten yards when he heard something, just the slightest rasping of breath. That would be King.

Fargo wondered again if King was expecting him or just resting. Fargo gripped the pick with both hands and took a step. The sole of his boot sluffed on the rock.

"Hello, Fargo," King said.

18

Fargo didn't wait to hear anything more. He swung the pick.

That turned out to be a mistake. In the darkness, Fargo had forgotten the low ceiling, and the pick clanked into it before it got to the top of its arch, sending a stinging vibration down both Fargo's arms.

Fargo held onto the pick and dropped to the floor, which was a good thing. He heard another pick or something similar whistle through the air right where he'd been standing.

It was a pick, all right. Its point hit the wall and bounced off.

"Where were you, Fargo?" King said. "I've been waiting."

Fargo pushed himself backward with both legs, sliding on the rough stone, hoping to put a little distance between himself and King, whose pick cut through the air again.

Again it hit the wall, and this time King was less pleased.

"Goddamn it, Fargo, you yellow son of a bitch, stand still and fight like a man."

Fargo stayed where he was. If King kept talking, Fargo could get a fix on him and do something pretty terrible to him with the pick.

King must have realized the same thing. He didn't say anything else, but Fargo could hear him breathing heavily. He wasn't used to swinging a pick. Fargo waited for him to move a little closer.

But King had also figured out that moving would be as dangerous as talking. He stayed where he was, and soon he had his breathing under control. Fargo could no longer hear him.

Several minutes went by. Fargo didn't mind waiting. He

could be patient when he had to. He wondered if King could do the same.

Apparently not. It wasn't long before Fargo heard the faint sound of movement, but King wasn't coming after him. Instead, the mine owner was leaving.

Fargo got to his feet. He didn't know why King had decided to give up on the fight, but it wouldn't do to let him get too far ahead, not now that they were so far away from an entrance. He was glad now that he hadn't hit King with the pick. He wasn't sure he could find his way out if King were dead. In fact, he was pretty sure he couldn't.

The darkness and the heat weighed down on Fargo again, and he let his mind wander. That was almost the end of him.

King hadn't gone far. He'd stepped into some kind of hollow in the tunnel wall and waited. Fargo would have had the point of King's pick through his middle if he hadn't heard King grunt just as he swung. Fargo was able to jump backward just in time to escape the blow. As it was, the point snagged on his shirt and tore through his buckskins. It took a layer of Fargo's skin along with it as well.

Fargo stumbled in the darkness and was suddenly disoriented. He stuck his pick in front of him just in time to meet King's next attack. The implements crashed together, and King pulled back, hooking Fargo's pick with his own and jerking it out of the Trailsman's hands.

Fargo's pick clattered to the floor, and King said, "That's the end of you, Fargo."

Fargo was confused and off balance. He blundered backward and tripped on a rock. As he fell, he felt the wind of King's pick pass by his stomach.

King cursed in frustration when the pick hit the wall. His yell was cut short when the wall cracked open with a sound like muffled thunder. Hot water gushed out and threw rock into the tunnel as the opening enlarged. The rock missed Fargo, but in seconds the water covered him where he lay, making him feel like a crawfish being brought to a boil.

He could no longer hear King, and he certainly couldn't see him. By the time he got to his feet, the water was up to his calves, rushing down the tunnel and threatening to knock him back down.

The water wasn't boiling, but it was very hot, and it was soon up to Fargo's waist, trying to suck him down. He tried to walk forward, but his feet were pulled out from under him by the water's relentless flow and he was swept under. He had time to catch a breath and hold it as he was dragged along the wall, bumping his head and shoulders. He reached out, and his fingers fought for a grip on the slippery rock. Finally they found a niche in the wall, and he held on with a grip like iron. His lungs were burning and his chest felt as if it might burst. He clawed himself upward, and his head broke through the surface. The hot water dragged at his clothes and almost removed his boots, but he held to the rock and took deep gasping breaths.

After a while the water level began to drop, slightly at first, but eventually it went down rapidly. Fargo was able to let go of the wall and stand up. He was glad the tunnel was sloping away from the direction he'd been headed. He was glad he hadn't been down there when the wall broke open.

He felt around in the water at his feet. He couldn't find the pick, and he wasn't going to take the time to look for it. He didn't know what had happened to King, but he'd been farther up the tunnel than Fargo, and the water probably hadn't been nearly as treacherous there. He'd probably figured that Fargo had drowned, but didn't hang around to find out. He'd kept on going wherever it was he'd been going in the first place.

So Fargo decided he'd go too. He knew which way was out, now. The water had clarified all that for him as it washed his confusion away. Nearly getting drowned would focus a man's attention if anything would. He dried his face with his sleeve and started sloshing his way upward.

He'd walked for about half an hour or more, when he saw a light ahead. He wondered how King had managed to hold onto his lantern until he'd gone a little farther and realized that the light was getting bigger and brighter. He was looking at another entrance to the mine. Or maybe it was the same place they'd entered. Fargo was still a little disoriented by his trip through the mine. There was no sign of King, and Fargo walked a little faster.

As he got closer to the opening, he blinked rapidly. The sun was still shining on Davidson Mountain, and the light was almost painful to Fargo's eyes after his having been in the darkness for so long. He slowed down and stood about ten yards from the exit, looking out at the trees and rocks, glad just to be able to see them. He was dirty and wet, but he was alive and out of the mine. He brushed at his clothes, but the sand clung to them. He decided it didn't matter.

King was nowhere in sight. He was probably halfway to California by now, unless he thought Fargo was dead. In that case he might have gone back to his mine to see who'd won the fight. Fargo hoped it was Wong and his men.

He edged closer to the daylight, being quiet and careful because there was another possibility. King might be lurking outside the entrance, waiting for Fargo to emerge.

But King was nowhere to be found. Fargo looked around for footprints, but the rocky soil gave no sign that King had ever been there. There was a squirrel chattering up in a tree, and a bluejay yammering back at him. The only other sound was the stirring of the leaves in the breeze.

Fargo stepped out of the mine and took a deep breath of the open air, filling his lungs, and let it out slowly. He heard something click against a rock and started to turn. He didn't make it around completely because King, who had been standing just above the entrance, landed on him like a small avalanche.

They went down together and rolled across the ground. King wound up on top, and rocks dug into Fargo's back and arms as King pummeled his face.

Fargo arched his back and threw King to the side. King scrambled to his feet and charged like a bull as Fargo rose. King's head buried itself in Fargo's midsection, and King wrapped his arms around Fargo, carrying him back to the ground.

This time Fargo landed so hard that the air was knocked out of his lungs. He gasped through his tight throat, but King got his forearm across it and cut off Fargo's air supply completely. Fargo felt like his head was swelling up to the bursting point. He thought his eyes might pop out and roll off his face.

King had his legs locked on Fargo's sides. He looked down at the Trailsman and said, "You're a hard son of a bitch to kill, Fargo, but this time I've got you."

Fargo thought King was too confident. His fingers fumbled

at his side for the Colt, and finally they found it. Fargo pulled the pistol and slammed it against the side of King's head. King's eyes glazed, but he didn't fall. His legs kept their grip, and his forearm bore down.

Fargo wasn't sure he had the strength to raise the pistol again, but it was either that or die.

He hit King again.

The pressure on Fargo's windpipe lessened, and he rasped in some air. Then he hit King a third time.

That did it. King went limp and collapsed atop Fargo, who shoved him off and stood up, still struggling to breathe. He holstered the pistol and stood bent over like a very old man, his hands on his knees as he drew in air through his burning throat.

After a while he straightened. King lay still nearby. Blood matted his hair and ran down the side of his face. Fargo walked over and nudged him with the toe of his boot, not exactly gently. King stirred and moaned, letting Fargo know he was alive.

The problem now was how to get him back down to the Silver King. Fargo looked around. There was a faint trail in the trees, and Fargo figured it led to the mine. He wouldn't have any trouble getting there, but he didn't feel much like carrying King. On the other hand, he didn't have anything to tie him up with, and he couldn't just leave him there. If he did, King would get away as soon as he came to.

Fargo thought about shooting him, but he couldn't shoot a defenseless man, even though that man had been trying to either kill him or have him killed for quite a while. Not to mention King's role in the beating he'd taken from Sullivan in the jail. Of course that could have been Sullivan's idea, considering how much the deputy marshal seemed to have enjoyed it.

Reaching down into his boot, Fargo unsheathed the Arkansas Toothpick and cut King's leather belt. Then he grabbed the bottoms of King's denim pants and pulled them off. The ground was going to be rough on King's ass, but Fargo didn't care. He slipped the knife back in his boot and cut the pants into strips. Then he used the strips to tie King's hands and feet. He dragged King over to a rock and set him up against it with his chin resting on his chest. King snored and snorted but didn't wake up.

Now that King was secure, Fargo was ready to go back to the mine. If Wong's gang had been victorious, everything would be fine. If they hadn't, well, Fargo didn't know exactly what he'd do. He hadn't planned for them to lose.

There was a rustling in the trees near the little trail, and Fargo looked up. Sullivan came out, holding a pistol and smiling.

"God save us, Fargo," he said. "Sure is a pleasure to see you again."

"Speak for yourself," Fargo told him.

"Oh, but I always do." Sullivan looked over at the rock where King sat, still out. "I see that our mutual friend Sam isn't doing much talking, however. I hope you haven't killed him Fargo. I'd hate to lose him and the mine and all we've worked so hard for."

"He's alive," Fargo said.

"That's good news, then. You're probably wondering how I got here, aren't you, bucko."

"No," Fargo said. "I figured you walked."

Sullivan laughed. It was a big, happy laugh, the laugh of a man without a worry in the world.

"I'm going to miss you, Fargo, truly I am," he said when he'd finished laughing. "It's not every man who can make me laugh like you can."

"I spread happiness wherever I go."

"That you do, Fargo, that you do. It's a shame I have to kill you."

"Why don't you quit talking about it and do it," Esmeralda said, stepping out of the trees. "I swear, Sullivan, sometimes I think you'd like to just talk people to death instead of shooting them."

Fargo had been wondering when Esmeralda would show up. "It was all planned from the start, wasn't it?" he said to her. "King told you he was going to lead me on a wild goose chase in the mine and try to kill me there. But he told you to get Sullivan and meet him here just in case he didn't succeed."

Esmeralda shrugged and tossed her black hair. She gave the unconscious King a disdainful look.

"It sure looks like he didn't succeed," she said. "I always knew he was soft."

"Be that as it may, darlin'," Sullivan said. "You had me and Slade to do the hard work for you. Sam did his job well, you have to admit."

"There's no *did* about it," Esmeralda said. "He'll keep doing it as long as I tell him. That is, he'll keep doing it if Fargo hasn't killed the bastard."

That little exchange was a revelation to Fargo. "Wait a minute," he said. "You mean it was your idea all along?"

"Of course it was," Esmeralda said. "Surely you didn't think Sam was smart enough to come up with an idea like that. He was going to give up the mine, but I talked him out of it and explained how he could make some money from it."

"And since you were getting rich," Fargo said, "you decided you might as well have all the saloon business in town, too."

"I deserved it. I didn't want to spend too much money too fast and make people suspicious, so I thought I'd do things the easy way. Run Marian off."

"Didn't work, though, did it," Fargo said.

"No, and if you had your way, you'd ruin everything. If those Chinamen have taken over the mine, it's ruined anyway." Esmeralda looked at Fargo with real hatred. "I can't believe you did that. But there's still a chance that Sullivan and I can salvage things. Go ahead and kill him, Sullivan. I'm tired of listening to him. He talks almost as much as you do."

Fargo thought that Esmeralda was the one doing all the talking, but he didn't think it would do any good to mention it.

"Why don't you put down the pistol and give me a chance," Fargo said to Sullivan. "We'll fight it out with our hands."

He thought the idea might appeal to Sullivan, given the man's brutal tendencies, but Sullivan wasn't interested.

"It sounds fine, Fargo, just fine, but there's always the chance you might win. A small chance, granted, but a chance nevertheless. So it's going to be shooting."

Fargo had been counting on Sullivan giving a long-winded response, and before Sullivan had quite gotten it out, Fargo had dived to the side, hit the ground in a rolling somersault, and come up near the rock where King was still propped up.

Sullivan was taken by surprise, and he snapped off two quick shots.

One of them plowed the ground in front of Fargo and sent dirt spurting up into the air.

The other one hit King in the same side of the head where Fargo had applied his pistol butt, but it had a much more severe effect. It blew out the other side of King's skull and splattered blood and bone all over the rock.

But by that time, Fargo was behind the rock and safe from Sullivan's bullets for the time being. He felt a little bad about King, who'd just happened to be in the way, but it wasn't Fargo's fault that Sullivan was a bad shot.

On the other hand, maybe he wasn't so bad. Maybe he'd hit exactly what he'd been aiming at. He might think that he and Esmeralda would make a good pair to run the mine with King out of the way, if Wong hadn't already taken over, that is.

Whatever Sullivan's motives, or lack of them, Esmeralda apparently didn't think killing King was a good idea at all. Fargo could hear her cursing Sullivan as two more shots whined off the rock that had been sheltering him. That made four shots total.

"Come on out, now, bucko," Sullivan called. "If it's a fair fight you want, it's a fair fight you shall have."

"I've changed my mind," Fargo yelled, checking his own pistol to make sure the water hadn't ruined the loads. He thought everything looked all right, but you could never be certain. And in a situation like this one, Fargo liked to be certain.

Esmeralda had stopped cursing Sullivan, and it was strangely quiet on the other side of the rock. Fargo wouldn't expect King to be making much noise, but when Sullivan stopped talking, he knew something was going on.

Fargo risked a quick look over the top of the rock. Sullivan and Esmeralda had disappeared.

19

Fargo heard the squirrel again. The blue jay was no longer around. The gunfire must have discouraged him.

Lowering himself back behind the rock, Fargo wondered where Sullivan and Esmeralda could have gone. They wouldn't have run away, and they wouldn't have left Fargo there if they hadn't had some kind of plan. They didn't want him to be alive and spreading the truth of what was going on with the Silver King.

So that meant they must be trying to slip up on him. Which side would they come from? Not from the front, because there was no one there. Or there didn't appear to be. One or both of them could be hiding in the trees, and Fargo wouldn't be able to see them. So he didn't think a dash for the path would be a good idea. He'd just have to wait where he was and see what happened. He figured he'd find out soon enough.

"Fargo! Fargo! Are you there?"

Fargo sat straight up. That wasn't Sullivan or Esmeralda calling him. It was Yee.

"Fargo! Where are you? Wong said to warn you that Sullivan was coming this way."

Fargo stayed where he was, wondering if this was some kind of trick. He leaned out around the rock and saw that Yee was standing at the edge of the trees. She seemed to have noticed King for the first time, and there was a look of revulsion on her face. She took a tentative step forward, and Sullivan came out of the trees behind her.

"And what a wonderful day it is for a walk in the sunshine," he said.

Yee whirled around, saw him, and started to run. But Esmeralda came out of nowhere and grabbed her with both arms around her waist. Yee kicked and twisted, but Esmeralda was larger and stronger and held her tight.

"Ah, and it's no use to struggle," Sullivan said. "We have you fair and square, you see."

"Foreign devils!" Yee said.

"Sure, and there's no good in calling us by your heathen names," Sullivan said. "Don't worry if she gets away from you, Esmeralda. If she does, I'll kill her."

"You weren't so good at killing Fargo," Esmeralda said.

"But he'll do what we tell him now, or we'll kill his lovely Chinese friend. Isn't that right, Fargo?"

Sullivan raised his voice for the last remark, but the Trailsman could have heard him anyway. Fargo stood up.

"Let her go, Sullivan," he said. "She doesn't have any part in this."

"Oh, but she does. She seems to know far too much, I'm afraid. You shouldn't have told her, Fargo."

"I didn't," Fargo said, knowing that Wong must have let her know their plans. He wished that she hadn't decided to get mixed up in them.

"Not that it matters," Sullivan said. "The end is the same."

He stood beside Esmeralda, who was holding Yee by both arms. Sullivan's pistol was pointed at Yee's head. Fargo knew he could draw and fire before Sullivan could shoot him. He might even be able to kill the deputy marshal, but Yee would most likely die, too, if Sullivan's finger tightened on the trigger.

"What do you want?" Fargo asked.

"I went you to take out your pistol and put it down on the ground. Then I want you to take two steps away from it and stand very still."

Fargo thought it over. It was a nice day, and he wasn't in any hurry to have it end in his death.

"You're trying my patience, bucko," Sullivan said.

Yee looked entirely defeated. Her head drooped down on her chest, and her hair hung in her face. In her baggy white pants and blousy shirt, she seemed fragile and helpless. Fargo knew that he had to do what Sullivan wanted, even though Yee would probably be killed anyway.

He was about to say he'd give in, when something happened. Fargo wasn't sure exactly what, since it was too fast for him to follow. There was a blur of motion, and at the end of it, Esmeralda was flying through the air. She landed on her back and didn't move.

Yee was several feet away from where she'd been standing, and Sullivan was so surprised that he seemed frozen in place.

Fargo was surprised, too, but he wasn't frozen. His pistol came out, and he fired at Sullivan, who was turning to face him.

The fact that Sullivan turned saved his life. Instead of going into the center of his chest, the bullet struck him in the meaty part of his shoulder, missing bone. His own shot tugged at Fargo's shirt near the ribs, and Fargo stumbled to the side.

Fargo shot again, but he was off balance, and the bullet went straight through Sullivan's neck. Blood pumped out, and Sullivan slapped his free hand on his neck to stanch the flow. It didn't help much. Sullivan continued to fire his pistol.

He must've reloaded, Fargo thought.

The bullets whanged off the rock near King's body but came nowhere near Fargo, and then the hammer clicked on an empty chamber.

Sullivan's eyes were unfocussed, and he looked around for Fargo.

"I'm right here," Fargo said.

Sullivan opened his mouth to answer, but no words came out. Just blood. Something had finally shut him up. The pistol fell from his limp fingers, as he stood there silently, dying.

Esmeralda sat up. She took in the situation in a glance, jumped to her feet, and ran.

Yee caught her easily and grabbed her by one arm. Esmeralda turned, her fingers clawed to scratch Yee's eyes out, and again Fargo couldn't quite tell what happened. The result was very similar to what had happened before, however. Emeralda sailed through the air and landed on the rocky ground. She didn't try to get up.

It was really something to see, but Fargo didn't think Sullivan had witnessed it, though he continued to stand where he'd been, and his mouth continued to move. There was no blood coming out of it now, only Sullivan's last gasps.

Fargo turned to Yee, "I never saw anything like that," he said. "How did you do it?"

Yee smiled. "In my country there is an art to fighting. Few women are taught the skills that I have."

"Can Wong do that?"

"Wong never cared to learn. I have another brother, still in China. He taught me."

"I'd like to learn that, myself."

"It takes years to become proficient. Wong never had the patience. I believe you would not like staying in one place long enough to learn properly."

She was right about that. Women always seemed to sense that Fargo liked to keep on the move, and that was fine with him. That way, they didn't try to stake any claims on him.

"What about the fight at the mine?" Fargo asked. "Is Wong all right?"

"We should go see. Things were going well when I came here. He saw the deputy marshal and the Gypsy Queen on a trail up the mountain, and he thought they might be coming for you. That is why he sent me."

"What were you doing at the mine in the first place?"

"I was there to fight. You have seen what I can do."

"I didn't see you there."

"I was dressed as a man. I seem to have lost my hat."

The shapeless clothing had concealed her figure, and the hat had hidden her hair. Fargo supposed it was possible that he hadn't noticed her.

"You shouldn't have put yourself in danger," he said.

"In this country," Yee said, "I am free to do whatever I please. That is one reason I am here."

"You're right," Fargo said, "and what you do is none of my business. Let's go see about Wong."

"What will we do with the Gypsy Queen?" Yee asked.

Fargo looked over at Esmeralda. She was disheveled, and there was dirt in her glossy black hair.

"You son of a bitch," Esmeralda said. "I think my ankle's broken. Help me up."

Fargo didn't respond. He turned his glance to Sullivan, who was somehow still standing. His mouth was closed and he was pale as the moon.

"Why don't you just give it up and die," Fargo said.

Sullivan opened his mouth. A final sound came out, but there were no words. It was just the ghost of a sigh. Then his knees buckled and he fell forward on his face. The only noise he made was the bump when he hit the ground.

Esmeralda looked at Sullivan and then at King. She must have realized that her situation wasn't good, no matter who won the fight at the mine. And it turned out that her ankle wasn't broken after all. She jumped up and ran down the trail.

Yee started to go after her, but Fargo said, "Never mind her. If you caught her, we'd just have to carry her back to the mine. She won't get far. She probably won't even try. I figure she'll just go back to her saloon and try to make out like none of this ever happened."

"Will the law deal with her?"

"Whatever law's left in Virginia City. Maybe things will be different without Sullivan around."

There were already flies buzzing around King's head. They'd be on Sullivan before too long.

"What about them?" Yee asked.

"We'll have to leave them here for the time being. Somebody can come get them later, if anybody cares."

"Then let us go see about Wong."

"Good idea," Fargo said.

Wong was in control. The miners had given up after the first assault, and Wong's men had herded them into the mine and kept them here at gunpoint.

Fargo congratulated Wong and said, "We need to get them out of the way before the shift change. We can round up the others when they come out of the mine."

"What will we do with them?" Wong asked. "The jail will not hold them all."

"You're right," Fargo agreed. "Hell, just let 'em go. They didn't kill anybody or rob any stagecoaches. They just kept King's secret. He was paying their wages, so you can't really blame them. Did you kill any?"

"No," Wong said. "It was an easy fight. But there are several wounded."

"See about getting them fixed up and let the others go. I appreciate your help on this."

"It was nothing," Wong said. "What will become of the mine now?"

"I don't know," Fargo said, brushing at his clothes.

"It will be abandoned," Yee said. "Like so many others. It was worthless from the start."

"It was turning a profit at the end," Fargo said.

"But illegally," Yee reminded him.

"Yeah, there's that. But you never know. Right now, I guess I'd better go to town and see what can be done about Esmeralda. Wong, meet me back at the Iron Dog later."

"I will be there," Wong said.

The back door to Esmeralda's office was locked, but after trying the knob, Fargo raised his foot and kicked the door right where the lock fit into the wood. The frame splintered, and the door flew open.

Esmeralda stood in the center of the room. She had changed into her saloon clothes, and she looked at Fargo with scorn.

"Why do you think you can break into my private room?" she asked. "Eet ess not permitted."

"Who's the act for?" Fargo asked. "Not for me. I know better."

"Sometimes I just slip into it without thinking. What are you doing here, you bastard?"

"I'm going to turn you over to the law for your part in the stage robberies," Fargo said. "I figure you knew about the killings, too, but maybe the law will go easy on you. It'd be hard to hang a beautiful woman."

"Nobody's going to hang," Esmeralda said. "I'm not even going to jail."

"There's too much evidence against you," Fargo said. "You're going, all right."

"No, I'm not. Because there's no evidence at all. There's only your word, and the word of some Chinaman. A Chinaman's word is worthless, and you're going to be dead, so who does that leave to testify?"

"Marian," Fargo said. "But I'm not dead, and I'm not going to be."

"Who'd believe Marian? She's been whining about me doing things to her saloon for so long, everybody will think it's just sour grapes."

"That still leaves me."

"Not necessarily. You never learn, do you?"

"Learn what?"

"To look behind the couch."

At her words, Glenn stood up. He was holding a pistol not much bigger than the one that had been in Fargo's soup.

"Hey, Fargo," Glenn said. "I'll bet you thought you'd never see me again. But Esmeralda likes me."

"I have to give you credit, Glenn," Fargo said. "You have more gumption than I thought."

"I have this gun, too. So long, Fargo."

Glenn pulled the trigger. Smoke puffed from the pistol.

The little bullet struck Fargo in the side and glanced off a rib. It knocked Fargo down, but he was back on his feet in seconds with his Colt in his hand.

"One shot's all you get," he told Glenn.

The piano player looked at the little pistol and dropped it to the floor.

"Don't kill me, Fargo," he said. "I was just doing what Esmeralda told me."

"So were Slade, King, and probably Sullivan," Fargo said.

He motioned to Esmeralda with the pistol barrel, indicating that he wanted her to go stand beside Glenn.

She spit at him, but then she went.

"Take off your suspenders, Glenn," Fargo said. "Tie her hands behind her back."

"I'll kill the little bastard if he tries it."

"You do, and I'll have to kill you," Fargo said.

Esmeralda spat again, but she let Glenn tie her hands.

"Now what?" Glenn asked.

"Now we go see who's in charge of the jail," Fargo told him.

That night, Fargo sat in the kitchen of the Iron Dog with Marian, Wong, Utley, and Carter. Fargo's ribs were bandaged tightly, but he could move around all right. One of them was probably badly bruised, he thought, but not broken.

Carter and Utley were relieved to hear that they were no longer in danger, and they found it hard to believe that the others had been killed for so little reason.

"King didn't think it was a little reason," Fargo said. "And neither did Esmeralda. They had a good thing, and they didn't want it messed up."

"Our mine has been messed up from the git-go," Carter said. "I've been trying to think we'll find something, but it don't look good. I'm about ready to pack up and go back to Missouri."

"Before you do that," Fargo said, "I have a proposition for you."

"What's that?"

"I think you should take over King's operation."

"What the hell?" Utley said. "You want us to take over a worthless mine? What're we gonna do to make it pay? Rob the stage?"

"I don't think you'll have to," Fargo said. "I've talked it over with Marian. She'll finance you to start with, so you'll have to split with her."

"That's right," Marian said. "I want a fair share."

"And I want Wong to be in on it, too," Fargo said.

"He's a Chinaman," Utley said.

"That is correct," Wong said. "Wong is just poor Chinaman. American gentleman is very observant."

"Stop that," Fargo said. "Utley, Wong's probably smarter than you and Carter put together. He can be a big help to you, and he can get some of his friends to work the mine. They need the money, and they'll work hard. You'll pay them a fair wage, too."

"Goddamn it!" Utley said. "I don't see how we can pay 'em if we don't have any money and if the damn' mine's worthless."

"That's what I was coming to," Fargo said. "I don't think it's worthless."

He told them how King had broken through the wall of the mine shaft with his pick. And then he told them about the sand that had clung to his clothing.

"Here's a little of it right here."

Fargo opened his hand and poured the sand on the table.

"I'll be Goddamned," Carter said.

Utley just stared.

"Blue," Fargo said. "I think King's shaft was just a few yards away from a vein. I think you fellas should work it."

"We'll do it," Utley said.

"What about Wong?" Fargo said.

"He looks like a fine partner to me," Carter said, and Utley nodded.

"Marian too."

"Sure," Carter said. "Anything you say, Fargo. But what about you?"

"I don't like staying in one place long enough to work a mine," Fargo said. "And I might be wrong about it. I don't want any part of it."

"Do you want anything at all?"

Fargo looked at Wong and said, "I've been half-drowned, shot, choked, and spit on today. What I need is some of that special soup Wong's sister fixes up. You reckon she's home, Wong?"

Wong smiled. "I would expect so, Fargo. Why don't you go see?"

Fargo stood up.

"I think I will," he said.

LOOKING FORWARD!

**The following is the opening
section from the next novel in the exciting
Trailsman series from Signet:**

THE TRAILSMAN #250
ARIZONA AMBUSH

*Arizona Territory, 1860—Where a woman's will is
not always her own, and the best things in life go to
the men willing to take them.*

She looked like trouble.

Luckily for Skye Fargo, she looked like the kind of trouble
he didn't mind getting into . . . in more ways than one.

"Buy a girl a drink, handsome?"

She was maybe twenty, probably younger. Her figure, en-
cased in a dancehall getup, curved in all of the right places.

The tall man in buckskins, known as the Trailsman, was
leaning against the bar of a place called The Bucket of Blood
in Quartz, Arizona Territory, nursing a lukewarm beer that
tasted like champagne, the way it cut through the trail dust that
parched his throat.

"Why sure, ma'am," he grinned. "What's your pleasure?"

She turned to the hovering bartender and ordered for herself. "The usual, Dave."

The mustached barkeep sauntered off.

Fargo was willing to bet that "the usual" was a shotglass of
water with a drop of brown food coloring to make it look like
whiskey. Fargo was no stranger to trail town honky-tonks like
this one and the women who worked the riders passing

through. He understood the rules of the game and was willing to play by those rules when the trail got lonesome.

Dusk was graying the windows of the barroom. Despite the fact that the bar was half full and rang to the laughter of men and some women, as well as to the tune of a player piano, Fargo felt that particular, aching loneliness of the trail that only a woman could cure.

The bartender brought the "shot" to the curvy redhead. Fargo paid him, and clinked glasses with her.

She smiled sweetly. "To new acquaintances."

As they sipped their drinks, Fargo's seasoned eyes openly assessed her. At no more than a hundred pounds, her height was a foot less than his. She was a cute little morsel. Curly red hair fell around a pretty, freckled Irish face of peaches-and-cream complexion, pouty red lips, and sparkling green eyes. The slightest layer of baby fat, and innocence in those vivacious eyes, only heightened the erotic effect of her lush young breasts pushed up and almost out of her plunging neckline.

And it was that sense of innocence that bothered Fargo, as did the circle of white around the fourth finger of her left hand. A wedding band had graced that finger until not very long ago.

But he was not a man to turn down an inviting smile from a beautiful woman. And the ride in from Yuma had been long and hard. He'd delivered the prisoner from Tucson to the prison as the territory, which depended on contract freelancers like himself for much of what little law enforcement there was in these parts, had hired him to. The prisoner had been convicted of killing a miner, as well as his wife and daughter, to gain hold of their claim and had tried to escape three times while in Fargo's custody. It had not been an easy job, and he was on his way back to Colorado where the weather suited him better this time of year. But the two-day ride thus far from Yuma had been brutally hot and dusty.

"What's your name, darlin'?" he asked this redheaded cutie.

Her smile was dimpled and cute as hell, but he could read human emotion as well as he could read sign on the trail, and

Fargo detected a hesitation within her, as if she were an actress still learning her lines.

"You can call me Desiree."

"Well, howdy, Desiree. You can call me Skye."

"Pleased to make your acquaintance." She finished the contents of her shotglass. "Buy me another?"

"I reckon." As he lifted an arm to summon the bartender, he added, "You're a mite young to be working in a place like this, aren't you, Desiree?"

Skye, you're a fool, he was telling himself. *Here you've got the sweetest little piece of goods you've seen in a long time, serving herself up to you for the price of a few drinks, and your damn conscience wants to get in the way . . .*

Desiree swallowed a quick gulp from the shotglass Dave brought her. "I'm old enough to know what I'm doing."

Fargo chuckled, taking another sip of his half-full beer that was becoming warmer by the second.

"Simmer down. I wouldn't be talking to you at all if I didn't think you were a grown woman who can make her own choices."

She blinked prettily, looking somewhat taken aback. "Well, thank you for that, at least."

"It's just that I can tell you're new at this," he added in a friendly tone. "I want you to do well in your new line of endeavor."

She looked flustered, standing there at the bar in her low-cut outfit. "You're making fun of me. That's not nice. And what makes you think this is a new line of endeavor?" she asked tartly.

"You don't want to use that tone," he advised. "You want to be polite to the boys who ride through looking for a night of female companionship. If they're looking for a thin-skinned shrew, they'll wait until they get back home to their wives or girlfriends."

She bristled. "Thin-skinned shrew? What makes you think—"

From behind them, a voice shouted, "Emma!"

Sudden silence descended upon the smoky barroom. Everyone made way for the man who had stomped in and now stood just inside, the bat-wing doors swinging behind him. Someone kicked the player piano and it stopped tinkering away.

The young man wore the coveralls and straw hat of a farmer. He wasn't armed, but his fists were clenched and his eyes were centered on the woman who stood next to Fargo. He stormed forward.

She whirled to face him. "Jed! What are you doing here?"

"I should ask you that question," he said in a firm, measured voice. He grabbed her by a wrist. "You're coming home with me, Emma. What the devil do you think you're doing in a place like this?" He stared around with disgust. "Why did you leave me, honey? I've been a day getting here. My God, I hope you haven't—" He couldn't complete the sentence.

"No, I haven't, Jed," she assured him in a peculiarly gentle voice that Fargo hadn't heard her use before. "Today is my first day, honest. I just started."

"Emma—"

"Jed, I swear that's the truth." She indicated Fargo. "This is the first gentleman who's bought me a drink. You never listen to me, Jed. You're always too busy with the crops and the figures in the ledger book. It's you who drove me away."

Jed didn't seem to hear her. And he didn't release his grip on her wrist. His glare swung to Fargo, utterly unimpressed by either the Trailsman's formidable size or by the formidable Colt holstered at Fargo's hip.

"So you thought you'd molest my wife, is that it, stranger?"

Oh hell, Fargo thought. He spoke in a reasonable voice. "First things first, friend."

"I ain't your friend."

"Whatever you say, Jed. Now unhand the lady."

"You watch your mouth, mister. This here's my wife. We're in love with each other, Emma and me. Ain't that so, honey?"

Her eyes lowered. "I do love you, Jed," she admitted. "But sometimes I don't know if you love me, or if you just think you own me. I thought I had to get away," she concluded in a choked voice, "but I . . . I don't know what I think."

"We've got ourselves a good home, a little farm a mile out of town," Jed told Fargo. "Until Emma went crazy day before last, that is. I'm here to bring her home."

"You're doing the right thing, Jed," said Fargo. "But you're doing it the wrong way." He nodded at the young man's white-knuckled hand that held her wrist like a vise. "Let her go, friend. Don't make me ask you again."

There was a hesitation. Jed looked into Fargo's eyes, and what he saw there made the farmer release his wife's wrist. But he glared at Fargo defiantly. "You oughta butt out and mind your own business."

Emma-Desiree massaged her sore wrist. She glanced in Fargo's direction, gratitude in her green eyes. "Thanks, mister. I'm sorry about this, really. I didn't know Jed was so, well, so hot-tempered."

"You go home with him," said Fargo. "Go back home and put on your wedding ring. You two have found love and that's something that seems to be in mighty short supply in this world." He indicated the smoky environment of the barroom. "This is my world, not yours. Give him another chance, Emma. I reckon he'll try a mite harder to understand. Right, Jed?"

Jed nodded eagerly, not sure what to make of the stranger but certain that they were in total agreement. "You listen to the man, honey. It won't be like it was before, I promise. I didn't know I'd miss you so much."

There was a moment of hesitation before she lifted her head, drew her shapely figure erect and spoke to him eye to eye. "All right, Jed. I'll try it with you again. This was a big mistake. Let's go home."

As they walked toward the bat-wing doors, Jed threw a backward glance over his shoulder in Fargo's direction. "Much obliged, mister."

Fargo acknowledged this with an index finger tip of farewell from the brim of his hat. "Good luck to you, sodbuster."

Emma-Desiree also sent him a look over her shoulder during that final instant before the little redhead and her husband disappeared from sight. It was a glance that Jed did not see.

Fargo was unable to read the look across the distance of the barroom, and he wasn't sure if anyone else saw it. He adored women but, like most men he knew, he barely understood them at the best of times.

Within heartbeats of the couple leaving, the player piano resumed its merry tinkling and the laughter and raucous rabble of the honky-tonk returned.

That was fine with Fargo. Feeling relaxed surrounded by the sounds of the bustling barroom around him, he turned back to the bar and finished his beer.

He became aware of a man standing next to him, a leathery-faced gent in his late fifties, stocky of build, wearing a duster over trousers, white shirt, and a jacket that bespoke financial success.

"Mr. Skye Fargo, I presume?" The man shouted to be heard above the barroom babble.

"Maybe," said Fargo, squinting. "Do I know you?"

"Not yet, but you'll want to."

"You sound mighty sure of yourself, mister. Why is that?"

"Because I have two things to offer you, which, if your reputation is accurate, you value more than anything in the world."

Fargo regarded the man with mingled skepticism and amusement. "And what might those things be?"

The man chuckled confidently. "Money and adventure," he said. "I can offer you an abundance of both, Mr. Fargo. I have a most intriguing story to tell you. I think it best if we find a table. May I buy you a drink?"

No other series has this much historical action!

THE TRAILSMAN

#225:	PRAIRIE FIRESTORM	0-451-20072-1
#226:	NEBRASKA SLAYING GROUND	0-451-20097-7
#227:	NAVAJO REVENGE	0-451-20133-7
#228:	WYOMING WAR CRY	0-451-20148-5
#229:	MANITOBA MARAUDERS	0-451-20164-7
#230:	FLATWATER FIREBRAND	0-451-20202-3
#231:	SALT LAKE SIREN	0-451-20222-8
#235:	FLATHEAD FURY	0-451-20298-8
#237:	DAKOTA DAMNATION	0-451-20372-0
#238:	CHEROKEE JUSTICE	0-451-20403-4
#239:	COMANCHE BATTLE CRY	0-451-20423-9
#240:	FRISCO FILLY	0-451-20442-5
#241:	TEXAS BLOOD MONEY	0-451-20466-2
#242:	WYOMING WHIRLIND	0-451-20522-7
#243:	WEST TEXAS UPRISING	0-451-20504-9
#244:	PACIFIC POLECOATS	0-451-20538-3
#245:	BLOODY BRAZOS	0-451-20553-7
#246:	TEXAS DEATH STORM	0-451-20572-3
#247:	SEVEN DEVILS SLAUGHTER	0-451-20590-1
#248:	SIX-GUN JUSTICE	0-451-20631-2

To order call: 1-800-788-6262